A Young Cowboy's Adventures

Stu Campbell

This is a work of fiction.

ISBN 978-0-9675164-7-9

Cover and text design by D.K. Luraas
Cover painting by Larry Jones, Bouse, Arizona
Author photo by Mark Gordon, Salt Lake City, Utah

Printed and bound in the United States of America

Contents

Heading Out   1

On the Trail   10

Surprise!   25

Rodeo   38

Another Surprise   57

A Change of Pace   73

On the Trail Again   124

Other Books by Stu Campbell

Horsing Around a Lot

Horsing Around the Dudes

Humor Around Horses

You Can't Be Serious!

Comedy Around the Corral

More Humor Around Horses

Heading Out

The job wasn't much. Look after a few cows, do some irrigating, fix some fence, it was hard to stay busy. Quite frankly, I was bored. I would have liked something more exciting. There wasn't much saddle time.

I would take my horse out to do the irrigating and fix fence. While I did the work, the horse would graze, peacefully hobbled. He was getting fat while I did the work. I know one time I went to get on my horse without taking off the hobbles—I was so bored I was forgetting things. I went to turn the horse and he didn't step out; he kinda reared. He couldn't move either foot more than four or five inches. I got off, undid the hobbles, got on, got the shovel and rode back to camp, very sheepishly. Although I was alone, I could still embarrass myself.

I could fix fence, I'd done plenty of that. The irrigating is what got me. Maybe I couldn't tell up from down, but I had a hard time getting the water to go where I wanted it to go. I'd have a whole bunch of water at the bottom of the field, yet at the top of the field, not twenty feet away from the ditch, I'd have a big dry area. Maybe I just didn't look at the ground right.

I wasn't doing a good job of everything, I knew it and the boss knew it. I could look after the cattle all right, but there wasn't much to look after. The cattle pretty much took care of themselves. Other than earmarking an occasional late calf, they all stayed healthy. The only chance I had to rope was when I spotted a slick calf that needed earmarking. While I was riding out checking the cattle, I did rope a lot of sagebrush, but I didn't think my roping was getting any better.

After a discussion with the boss when he brought up some groceries, we mutually decided on parting ways after the hay was cut and put up. That meant I'd have to cut the hay, bale it, haul it, and stack it by myself. That didn't bother me so much; it meant another week or two of work, a little more money, then I could go and do what I pleased.

As soon as I could, I stopped irrigating. Maybe there was something wrong with the shovel … every time I let go of it, it would fall over. I was relieved the irrigating was over. I really didn't know how to do it and didn't like it very much anyway. When the ground dried out, I started to cut hay.

I'd always liked mowing hay. The smell of new mown alfalfa hay was very pleasing. I had a hay mover mounted on the side of the tractor and I enjoyed watching the hay lay over as I cut it. A feller could go pretty fast, and the faster he went the faster the hay laid down. The raking was pretty simple, just go up and down the field with a side delivery rake and rake the hay into windrows. I figured it out that if I put two windrows into one, I wouldn't have to walk as much when it came time to pick up the bales and put them on the trailer.

The baling was a different matter. It was dusty and dirty, and because I'd put two windrows into one, I couldn't go as fast. I plugged up the baler once and had to stop everything and unplug it. I baled the hay a little slower after I unplugged the baler. It also made a lot of noise. But I got the baling done. All that was left was to put the trailer on the tractor, load the hay and stack it in the stack yard.

This was the hardest part of the job. It involved quite a bit of muscle, lifting the hay bales onto the trailer, trying to stack them from the ground so I wouldn't have climb on the trailer, put the bale in place, then get down and get the next bale. I decided not to stack the bales six or seven high, I would just go as high as I could get the bales on without me getting on the trailer, then go to the stack yard and unload them.

The bales had come out of the baler and generally landed on the wide side of the bale. I had learned from some of the older hands to roll the bale over toward me once or twice before picking it up. Quite often there would be a rattlesnake coiled up under the bale and if a feller just lifted the bale up without moving it, he might get bit. A lot of bending over was involved, causing a lot of back work, but it was better than getting bit by a rattler. It was work!

When I'd get a little tired, I'd take a break by saddling a horse and riding out to check the cows. I thought this was a good plan, because I was staying busy and doing something constructive at the same time. But I finally got the hay hauled and stacked.

It was time to leave. I hadn't given much thought to getting home in time for school to start. I figured I would catch a bus. I didn't have a car, actually I didn't even have a driver's license— I wasn't old enough to drive. All I had to take with me was my saddle, saddle blankets, a pair of chaps, a bridle, a bedroll, and some extra clothes. I didn't have a lot of luggage.

I was in for a surprise when it came time to settle up.

"I don't have enough money in cash to pay you," the boss said.

"I'm stranded," I said, "if I don't have enough money for a bus ticket. An' if that's all I got enough money for, I ain't had a profitable summer. I won't even have money for new school clothes."

"Well, I'll give you what cash I got, then give you what you want from the ranch as the balance. That should square us up. You can take what we trade to town and sell it for more cash, an' I'll even give you a ride to town an' help you sell it."

I got to thinking that the old man might be trying to get to me, taking advantage of a young teenager. I thought I'd have to do some pretty sharp trading to come out ahead for the summer's work.

"I'd sure like to have that little horse I've been riding," I said. I'd been riding a little sorrel horse that didn't get used much. He was undersized and had a Roman nose. He really wasn't much to look at, but he was gentle, easy to catch, and I'd taken a liking to him.

"I can sure trade you for that little horse, but you can't get him on the bus with you," said the boss. "That little horse don't get used much anyway."

"I don't figure on ridin' the bus," I said. "If I trade you for that horse, I'd ride him home, then sell him when I get there. 'Course, I'd need some extra gear to make it home."

"Like what?"

"Some cooking gear, groceries, a pack horse, pack saddle, pack bags …"

"You mean panniers," interrupted the boss.

"Yea, I guess so." I was pretty green and didn't really know the proper terminology. But I knew what I needed.

"How long will it take you to get home?"

"If I can make ten miles a day, I can make it by the time school starts," I replied.

4

Actually, I wouldn't be bothered if I missed some school, I really wasn't a premier student and didn't enjoy it much.

"What will you do for cooking?"

"Since I been workin' for you, I been doin' my own cookin'." I replied. This was true and even though I'd lost some weight, I did avert getting hungry or even starving to death. Admittedly, I wasn't the best cook.

"So you figure on ridin' home?"

"Yep," I replied.

"I don't think you can make it," said the boss.

I was surprised at this apparent concern regarding my welfare. I had kinda thought that the boss didn't much care for me.

"I can make it," I replied. "I've got plenty of time, it's an easy ride an' I think it might be kinda fun. That's what I'll do."

"You've got your mind made up? You've thought about this?"

I hadn't really given it much thought, it was a spur of the moment idea, formulated to get as much as possible from the boss to make up for the difference in wages I might miss out on.

"I'll need a pack horse," I said, changing the subject. I became a little enthused about this new adventure and was anxious to get started. "How's about that two-year-old paint colt you got for a pack horse? The trip will do him a world of good an' he'll be plumb gentle by the time I get home."

"That colt is goin' to be too good a horse when he grows up to trade him off now," said the boss. "That old bay mare would probably work better for you."

"No," I said, "That old mare wouldn't make the trip. She'd probably die before I got home. I need something in better shape, something more sound."

I thought if the old mare died on the trail, I might look like a gypsy traveling around the country with a bedroll tied behind the saddle and various cooking utensils tied to the saddle. Even though I was going to be traveling alone, I was very conscious of what I would look like. And the thought of a frying pan getting caught on some brush and slamming against the horse's flanks and getting me bucked off in the middle of nowhere was not very inviting.

Having this thought did do some good. I would need some cooking gear, at least a frying pan and a small pot. A coffee pot would be nice, too. I had almost forgotten these items with my spur of the moment thought.

"Well, the only thing I got that I don't really need or have a use for is that burro. She's due to foal in a couple of weeks, but I really don't have a use for her. She could make your trip."

"I really ain't much interested in the burro," I replied.

"Take it or leave it," said the boss.

"What's she bred to?"

"I don't really know," replied the boss. "It could be one of the young, wild studs runnin' around here or it might be one of the wild burros out on the desert. She came up missing a year or so ago and finally just came wandering back to the ranch. But you better take her, it's her or nothing."

I thought he was starting to get a little peeved and I still needed a pack saddle and some groceries. I didn't want to press my luck, so I accepted her.

"Now I need some groceries an' a pack saddle," I said.

"There's an old pack saddle in the barn," replied the boss. "It fits the burro, we used to use it on her when we used her. And the panniers, or as you call 'em, pack bags, are hangin' with it."

"Now I'll need some groceries an' something to cook with." I was repeating myself to make sure I got what I wanted.

"You can get that from the supply house an' check with the

cook to get an old fryin' pan an' a pot. Only get a week's worth of groceries, I ain't goin' to feed you for all summer when you only worked half the summer!"

Knowing I had pushed the boss about as far as I could and wanting to make the best deal I could, I settled for it. But I added one item, "I'll need a halter an' lead rope for the donkey."

"The halter we used on the burro is hangin' with the pack saddle. You can have it. There's some old lash ropes there, you can have them. Get your stuff an' meet me at the house, I'll pay you what you got comin', less all this equipment."

I went to the corral, caught my Roman-nosed sorrel horse, saddled him and then caught the burro. I went to the barn, got the pack saddle, panniers, and halter and went to catch the burro. There were some old saddle blankets with the pack saddle and I appropriated them.

I saddled the burro and went to the cook to get groceries and cooking supplies. Some coffee, canned pork and beans, canned beef stew, some vegetables and canned stewed tomatoes; I figured this would do the trick, for a while anyway.

As I gathered the groceries, I loaded them in the panniers, trying to get the weight as even as possible. When I had one pannier loaded I put it on the burro then went to putting some more supplies in the other pannier. While I was doing this, the burro started raising a fuss, and trying to buck the half loaded pack saddle off.

I was a little perplexed. What was happening?

The cook was watching from the porch of the cook shack.

"Better get both panniers loaded then get them on the burro," he said. "With that one pannier on one side, it's pinchin' her, an' she's mighty uncomfortable! She'll buck off the whole load before you get done!"

Kinda embarrassed, I went to the burro and took off the pannier. I straightened the pack saddle, tightened the cinch and loaded the other pannier. I had learned something, and I didn't know whether the cook had taught me or if the burro had.

I got the other pannier loaded, got the bedroll tied on top, and was ready to go to the house to get paid.

Much to my surprise, the boss was down at the corral with cash money in his hand to pay me. I suppose he was as anxious for me to leave as I was to go.

"Here's your cash. I think we're pretty even with all that I threw in on the deal."

"I do need a bill of sale on the horse and burro and the pack saddle. They all have your brand on 'em, an' I don't want to be accused of stealin' 'em," I said.

The boss wrote out a bill of sale on my animals and gave it and the money to me. He also gave me half an old pencil.

"What do I want that for?"

"You might want to make some notes," replied the boss.

I took the cash without counting it; put it and the pencil in my shirt pocket and said, "Thanks."

"Good luck to you," said the boss.

Once again I was surprised at this apparent display of concern.

We shook hands, I gathered up the lead rope to the burro, got on my horse and started out.

The burro was reluctant to move, so I dallied up and started to drag her. The boss gave her a good slap on her rump, and with a buck or two, we started out. I felt lucky that the pack didn't shift and we didn't lose the whole thing.

"Sometimes she's a little slow to get started an' needs some encouragement," hollered the boss. "But once you get started, she'll just follow along, gentle as a lamb."

I was starting to have a little misgiving, but didn't want to show any lack of confidence in front of the boss or the cook. I started down the road to the highway and I think the boss and the cook were both a little surprised when I turned up the road rather than down the road toward town.

On the Trail

Traveling down the highway was uneventful. Leading the burro was kinda slow and at her slower pace, I had to constantly either jerk her to keep her up to pace or slow my horse down. My horse was a pretty fast walker, a trait I looked for and enjoyed in a horse. The burro was slow. I'd have to find a happy medium and decided I'd have to increase the burro's speed as I didn't want to slow the horse down any.

I kept well to the side of the highway, off in the barrow pit. The few cars that went by didn't seem to slow down any as they passed by and I didn't want to get hit and run over. A few of the cars did slow down, and I thought I saw some people taking my picture as they passed.

I suppose we did make a sight traveling down the barrow pit. I didn't know what kinda time we were making, but it was slow. I was constantly having to jerk the burro and was becoming frustrated with her. As I jerked her, I started to cuss her. I was using words I had only heard the older hands use and wasn't really sure of their meaning.

It occurred to me that I hadn't found out the name of the

burro and decided to give her one. I certainly couldn't keep calling her what I had been calling her.

"What would be appropriate?" I said, thinking out loud. I didn't know it, but that was to become a habit on this trip. "Ass? After all, she is one and that might be suitable. But it might not be appropriate. How's about Lady Ass? That still might not work."

I was having a little trouble thinking up a name for the burro.

"I could call her 'Caesar.' No." I said to myself, "Caesar won't do."

I'd always wanted a horse named Caesar because I thought Caesar was a great man and any horse I owned would certainly be a great horse. Well, this burro I now owned certainly wasn't a great horse and never would be, so Caesar wouldn't work.

However, thinking about Caesar did cause me to name the horse. It occurred to me that I'd never named the Roman-nosed horse I now owned. I'd always just called him Boy.

"Maybe I should name you Caesar," I said to the horse. "I could call you Caesar an' the burro Cleopatra! I don't think that would work. Maybe Mark Anthony an' Cleopatra would be better! No, she ain't that good lookin' a burro an' I'm not sure how good a horse you really are.

"But we're on a Roman kick an' you got that Roman nose, I'll just call you Roman! Yep, that would work. Now, what about a name for the burro? I sure can't keep callin' her what I been callin' her. How about Sally? It's plain an' simple, just like she is."

So I named my critters, although I didn't always call them by their given names, particularly Sally.

The trip down the highway the first day was uneventful other than a few passengers in the cars that would wave. Without thinking, I would wave back. I had no idea when I started out that this would be a sociable trip.

As I traveled, it occurred to me that it was past noon, and I hadn't eaten anything. I was starting to get a little hungry. However, all my foodstuffs were packed on the burro, Sally that is. To stop and unpack Sally, cook up something to eat, then repack would cost me time, and I didn't really have that many groceries. I did have the time. But I wanted to keep going. I would forgo a noon meal and remember to keep something out for the next day.

Early on in the afternoon, I started to look for a place to make camp. I wanted water, grazing, firewood, and I wanted to be away from the highway.

About three in the afternoon, I started looking for a campsite. I did know of a creek with some grass ahead and there was even a gate to get into the pasture. I decided to use the creek and make camp. Even though there was still a lot of daylight left, I'd have plenty of time to hobble Roman and make camp. I didn't know what to do with Sally. I wasn't sure she'd stick around if I just turned her loose.

I found a spot far enough from the highway where I couldn't be seen, and made camp. It was a nice spot, a creek running by, plenty of grass, a little clearing surrounded by aspen trees. It belonged to the outfit I had just left and I felt a little uneasy about camping on the ex-boss's property, but it was a good spot. I hoped if he found out, the ex-boss wouldn't mind.

I unsaddled my horse, hobbled him and turned him loose. I hoped he'd stay close to camp; he always did at the camp where I watched the cattle, irrigated, and put up hay. I was wishing I had some grain to give him, as a little grain at night and a little in the morning would help keep him close to camp.

Next I unpacked Sally. She kicked me in the leg after I lifted off one pannier and walked around her rump to get the other pannier.

"Better keep an eye on her," I said to myself, as I lifted off the pannier. "Maybe I should have unpacked her first. I'll try that tomorrow; maybe she's tryin' to teach me some manners, her bein' a female."

I didn't really know what to do with her, I didn't want to turn her loose, she might leave. The lead rope on the halter wasn't long enough to allow her to graze during the night and get enough to eat. I decided to use my thirty-three-foot long lariat rope and tie it to the lead rope. This would give her at least a sixty-six foot circle to graze in during the night and the lead rope would add another ten or twelve feet. I didn't much like the idea of tying a knot in my lariat, but I figured it wouldn't hurt it if I tied it on the end away from the honda. Then I decided to tie a big knot in the lead rope after I passed it through the honda of the lariat rope. I did this, gave it a tug and it held. I saved my lariat rope.

Next, I started to gather some firewood. As I went about this task, I got to thinking that it might have been wise to commandeer an axe, or at least a hatchet. There were plenty of dead aspen limbs lying around, but it would have been easier to have an axe. One good cut in a sizeable aspen limb will make it fairly easy to swing the limb against a rock or tree trunk and bust it about the right size for a campfire. Trying to bust the limbs against a rock or whatever without the cut to weaken it was a little difficult. Knowing that aspen burns fast, I gathered up quite a bit, needing it for cooking supper and again for breakfast in the morning.

As I gathered up the firewood, I realized how much I had taken for granted as I started out on my trip. I wished I had an axe, I wished I had grain for the horse and burro, and I was to find myself wishing I had got a lot more standard supplies.

I spread out my groceries after I got the fire going. "Now let's see, what shall I have for supper? I have a choice between beef

13

stew and pork and beans. I guess I'll have the beef stew, as it's as close to prime rib as I got, an' on my first night out, I'll go high on the hog."

I was wishing I'd have gotten a can opener as I opened up the stew. I knew my pocketknife wasn't very sharp and to keep opening the tin cans with it would dull it real quick. I made a mental note to buy a can opener when I passed through a small town.

The beef stew tasted mighty good after missing the noon meal, and after it got hot, it didn't stick around very long. One of those cans doesn't look very big on a shelf, but they're sure filling at suppertime. As I washed the pot in the creek, I got to wishing I had some dish soap. It took quite a bit of scrubbing to get the pot clean, I'd scorched the pot while cooking the stew. I decided I needed to stir the pot a little more frequently to make housecleaning chores easier.

"Housecleaning chores," I said to myself. "This ain't no house! These are camping chores, but not housecleaning chores. I need to remember where I am!"

I chuckled at myself for my apparent aim at being proper. "What difference does it make? I'm out here alone!"

Being able to laugh at myself made the beginning of this trip more bearable. As I finished cleaning the pot, I thought to myself, "If I had a pair of pliers, I could cook this stuff right in the can and not have to do all these housekeeping chores! That is, camping chores!"

I smiled again as I corrected myself. I took the pot back to camp then took my coffee cup down to the creek to get a drink of water and wash down supper.

"I probably ought to have a canteen on this trip. A drink of water might come in handy during the hot afternoon. I really didn't plan this very well … I need a canteen, a can opener, grain for my horse and Sally, dish soap, a hand axe, an' probably a lot of other stuff. Nope, I didn't plan this as good as I could have."

As I laid out my bedroll on the softest looking grass I could find and started to get ready to hit the sack, I had another sudden thought: "Toilet paper! I'd forgot that, too. No I didn't plan this trip very well!"

I laid down to just relax some before I went to bed. The sun was just going down and I figured there was about a half hour before it got dark. As I laid there making a mental list of what I should buy at the first little town I came to, I heard a truck coming toward me.

I'd heard some of the traffic out on the highway, the bigger trucks catching a lower gear as they rounded the curve and headed up the hill. But this truck didn't sound like a big semi catching a gear; it had a strangely familiar sound to it. I'd heard it before. I wondered what kind of trouble I was going to get into with uninvited visitors showing up on my first night on the trail.

There was just enough light when I saw the pickup, then I recognized the truck. It was my ex-boss!

"I wonder what he wants. He'll probably throw me off his property, an' that'll be a chore, getting' packed an' loaded in the dark. I'm not goin' to like that much," I said, thinking out loud again.

"How you doin', son?" The ex-boss sounded strangely friendly as he got out of the pickup. I really wasn't sure what he had on his mind and was a little leery.

"I'm doin' all right," I replied. I was sitting on my bedroll, playing with an aspen twig as I spoke.

"I got to thinkin'," he said, as he walked to the rear of the truck, "you might need some of this to keep your horse an' burro close to camp."

From the back of the truck, he lifted a sack of grain.

"It's rolled oats with some cracked corn. Give some, just a little, about two or three handfuls in the morning an' the same amount in the evening, an' your livestock will be close to camp when you wake up in the morning."

"I hadn't given that much thought," I said. "I surely do thank you for it. What do I owe you?"

"Nothin'. I just got to thinkin' an' thought you might need it. The Missus also sent these."

He pulled a box of matches off the front seat of the truck.

Matches! That's something I needed and I hadn't given it any kind of thought, even though I had just used most of mine up a bit ago lighting the fire. I surely hadn't given enough thought to my preparations in my spur of the moment decision.

"Anything else you need?"

"I think I'm all right," I answered. I didn't want him to know that I hadn't fully thought out this plan.

"Looks like you're set up pretty well," said the ex-boss. All during our brief conversation he'd been surveying my setup, from the pile of firewood to the hobbled saddle horse and the burro tied to a tree with plenty of lead rope so she could graze.

"Yep, you're set up all right. I'll be headin' out," said the ex-boss.

"I sure thank you for the grain an' the matches. I'll pay you for them, if you want."

The ex-boss waved a hand as a "no" reply, got in his truck, turned it around and drove off. "Keep your matches dry, an' put out your fire," was all he said.

I opened the grain sack, took out a double handful of grain and walked toward Sally.

"Here you old witch. Maybe you won't kick me tomorrow if I feed you this little treat tonight. Don't you bite me!"

I let the burro finish the grain then got a double handful for Roman.

"Ol' Pard, I'll give you more of this if you'll be close in the morning."

I didn't have much fear of the little horse wandering off too far. The hobbles were good, there was plenty of feed and water close by, there wasn't much reason for the horse to go too far.

Water! I had Sally tied, but too far from the water. I tied her to another tree where she could reach the water on her own, rather than me having to lead her to water. It occurred to me that I was learning some, even on my first day.

Contented that everything was all right, I put some more wood on the fire, pulled off my boots and got ready for bed. It was already dark. What there was of a moon that night was coming up over the hill to the east. I laid there in my bedroll looking at the stars and fell asleep.

I woke up the next day after the sun was up. I didn't know what time it was, I didn't have a watch, but I figured it was around six, maybe six-thirty. It took me a minute to get my bearings, to remember where I was and what I was doing. When I finally became fully awake, I hurriedly checked my horse.

Roman wasn't far from camp, peacefully grazing close to the creek. Sally was still tied and had tromped down a lot of the grass in her seventy-some odd foot circle. There was still a lot of feed in her circle and I was sure the lead rope and lariat combination had given her ample room to graze at night.

I started to give some thought to breakfast for me. What should I have? The menu was the same as the night before, beef stew or pork and beans. I could open a can of vegetables and make do with that. I pondered the situation as I got water from the creek and made some coffee. I really wasn't much interested in eating, I was more anxious to get moving.

I lingered over my coffee, anxious to get going but giving my plans some serious thought. I knew the country around this area fairly well, but another day or two of riding along the highway would put me on Forest Service land. I would have to find a trail to get through the forest, but I'd have to have plenty of water along the way.

I saddled Roman as he ate a double handful of grain. When he finished, I bridled him and left him hobbled while I repacked my panniers. I kept out a can of stewed tomatoes for a noon meal, remembering yesterday's episode after the noon mealtime had passed. Then I saddled Sally and quickly loaded the panniers before she could raise a ruckus. I untied the knot in the lead rope, coiled my lariat and fastened it on my saddle. I was ready.

Satisfied that all was good, I took the hobbles off Roman, gathered up the lead rope on Sally, got on the horse and started to leave. As I rode out of camp, I noticed the fire was still smoldering.

I got off Roman, hobbled him, tied Sally to a tree, found the empty beef stew can, and went to the creek for water to fully put the fire out. It took a couple of trips, but the fire was dead out. I wasn't ready when I thought I was. I put the empty beef stew can in one of the panniers, took the hobbles off Roman, untied Sally, got on my horse, and had a final glance at what had been my home for one night, to make sure I hadn't left anything, and I rode off.

The trip along the highway was once again uneventful and I had a lot of time to think.

"That was sure nice of the ex-boss to bring the grain yesterday." I was talking to myself again, although Roman did show some interest in my comments with his ears.

Noticing Roman's interest in my comments, I continued out loud, "Maybe the ex-boss likes me more than I thought, he did bring me grain. 'Course I really can't use it, it's more for you an' Sally."

I glanced at Sally over my shoulder to see if she was paying attention. She wasn't paying attention, just plodding along, grabbing a mouthful of grass every now and then.

"I won't include you in this conversation if you don't pay attention, Sally!" The burro still didn't have a reaction.

"I suppose, because the grain is for you, the ex-boss probably thinks more of you than he does me. That's no matter, we're done with that."

For the most part, riding along the highway was kinda boring. Watching the cars go by became the most interesting pastime. Occasionally a passenger would wave at me and I felt obliged to wave back. When there were kids in the car, they would watch me until they were out of sight. I would volunteer a wave at them just to see if they would wave back. I noticed there were a lot of out-of-state cars on the highway. "Vacationers," I thought.

At one point, a car stopped and waited for me to catch up to them. There were three kids that piled out of the car along with their parents. I approached them wondering if I was in trouble.

"Can we take your picture?"

I was a little surprised. I had never thought of myself as a celebrity. I suppose we did make an interesting sight.

"I suppose," I said.

At once the kids made a mad rush towards Sally.

"Stop," I shouted. "Stay away from the burro! Just yesterday she kicked me an' I don't know how kid friendly she is!"

The kids stopped just short of Sally when the dad hollered at them upon hearing my warning. They lined up in front of Sally, far enough away to be out of kicking distance and got their picture taken. The kids really wanted to pet Sally, but I thought better of it. I didn't want to see any kid get kicked, and I could still feel the dull ache where Sally had kicked me the day before. And I didn't want to get off my horse and get back on for a picture.

I explained to the parents my reluctance to let the kids get too close to Sally. The kids weren't listening very well; all sorts of questions were coming at me before I could even answer one.

The most common questions were, "Can we feed her?" They asked that question a number of times, even though Sally didn't look like she was starving.

"That might not be too good an idea," I replied. Sally was busy eating all the grass she could and I didn't want to get off Roman. Roman started grazing while we were stopped, too.

The dad went to the car, got a couple of apples and said, "You can give these to the burro and horse when you stop later." Then, reaching into his wallet, he pulled out a five-dollar bill and handed it to me.

"This is for you," said the dad.

"Thanks," I said, taking the bill and putting it in my shirt pocket.

When I put the bill in my pocket, I realized I had the cash for my wages in that pocket. I hadn't even counted it. I thought I had better count it after the people left. I had no idea how much money I had, and I'd been making plans to get more supplies.

When the tourists left, I continued traveling down the barrow pit, letting Sally grab a mouthful of grass occasionally. She seemed to be keeping up a little better. I pulled out my pocket-knife and cut one of the apples in half.

"I probably ought to help you with these apples," I said, thinking out loud. "I really wouldn't want you to get a belly-ache."

That apple really hit the spot, not having had any breakfast that morning. I decided to pick up some apples when I hit a store somewhere. They made a pretty good snack.

I figured it was close to one o'clock when I decided to stop and have my can of stewed tomatoes for a noon meal. I found a shady spot, hobbled Roman and took off his bridle. I tied Sally low to a tree to allow her to graze some, and opened my tomatoes.

We had a nice lunch stop, all three of us getting something to eat. I decided to eat the second apple myself, as the horse and burro were busy in the grass. Feeling somewhat guilty because the apples were supposed to be for the horse and burro, I quartered the apple with my knife and ate it. I still felt guilty as I drank the juice from the tomatoes, but I got over the guilt quickly.

With some food in my stomach, a nice shady spot with plenty of grass for the horse and burro, I thought a rest might be appropriate, perhaps even a little nap. I felt fairly contented, but really didn't get any sleep. I've always found it tough to fall asleep during the middle of the day.

But the rest in the shade was relaxing.

After an hour or so, we started out again. I got to thinking that I should start looking for a place to camp early, so I could set up camp in the daylight. That became a routine every day, find a place to camp, unpack Sally and stake her out, unsaddle and hobble Roman, then gather firewood and set up my camp. I followed the same routine every day and didn't get kicked by Sally. I enjoyed watching the sun go down after supper, and the fire die down.

Every time we crossed a little stream, I would pause and let Roman and Sally drink their fill. Often, I would get off and get a drink myself; I didn't have a canteen to carry water in.

The third day on the trail did bring some excitement. I was still going along the highway in the barrow pit when a highway patrolman stopped in front of me, turned on his overhead lights, got out of the car and waited until I got to him.

"Running away from home, son?" The patrolman sounded very businesslike.

"No, sir, I ain't. I'm sorta runnin' at a slow walk *back* to home." I thought my answer and the way I phrased it was funny. The highway patrolman didn't. I grinned at my reply, the cop didn't.

"Where are you going?"

"Home," I answered, deciding to avoid the humor. I was going to ask him if he was going to give me a ticket for speeding, but decided against it. He didn't seem to be in very good humor.

"Where's home?"

The cop had a lot of questions and I didn't know why he stopped me. I suppose he was just doing his job.

I told him my situation, what I had been doing and where I was going, and how I planned to make the trip, trying to take advantage of free feed for my horse and burro along the road and eventually in the forest.

I asked him, "Why all the questions?"

The cop relaxed a little, and shed some of his businesslike demeanor.

"It's part of the job to check on all the vagrants in the area," he replied.

I didn't know I was a vagrant. I was just between jobs and had some money, that I still hadn't counted, and I had a plan.

The cop and I talked for quite a while and I began to feel a little more comfortable. The cop began to ease off his business-like manner and became human. I didn't know it, but during our conversation, he was searching for a statute that he could bring me in on. While there may be statutes governing kids running *away* from home, there appear to be none regarding kids running *back* to home.

Before the patrolman let me go, I got some directions on how to get through the forest to the next town. The directions were very helpful; he knew where the campsites and water were. One particular piece of information he gave me was most helpful.

He said, "Don't take the first forest service road you come across. That's a dead end road, and while you can take a trail over the top, it's a tough trail on both man and horse. The trail down the other side is closed due to an avalanche and a lot of fallen trees. You probably can't make it horseback. I know, I shot an elk up there three years ago and it took us four days to get him out. Take the second forest road up to the end then take the first trail to the right, the sign says, 'Moon Lake.'

"Follow that trail over the top and stay on it all the way down to the pavement. You'll come to the southeast part of town, close to the fairgrounds. That's where you can keep your horse and burro overnight."

"How long will it take to go over the mountain?" I asked.

"It'll take you about three days," replied the cop.

"How many days to go around on the highway?"

"It's about fifty-five or sixty miles on the road. It's all fenced and you'll have a hard time finding a place to camp off the road. Water might be a problem. You'll do better to follow my directions."

"I'll do that," I said, "You're the cop."

He didn't much care for me calling him a "cop," but he made me repeat the instructions, and I did ... he was the law.

He finally let me go, not having a valid reason to take me in, with a friendly warning, "There's a rodeo in town and you should be getting there just about the time it's going on. Be careful, there are some pretty rough cowboys come in off the ranches for the rodeo, don't get yourself in trouble! Good luck!"

I was glad the cop had given me some good directions. When I got to the first forest service road, I would have taken it, it looked pretty inviting. I could see some aspens and a small stream close to the highway.

The second forest service road didn't look as inviting as the first, but I took it. After a mile or so, I started riding through some aspen groves and I started looking for water to make camp.

Surprise!

Making camp was the same routine every day. Each day was the same because the country and scenery doesn't change much with a day's horseback riding. I was starting to get tired of my regular meals of beef stew or pork and beans, and decided to get some variety in my groceries when I got to town.

After I fixed supper, I pulled out the pencil my ex-boss had given me and on the back of the bill of sale I had, I started to make a list of the grocery items I wanted to get when I got to town. I'd lost track of how many days I had been out on the trail, but the way my groceries were being used up, I figured I'd better get into a town within the next couple of days.

I inventoried my remaining supplies and thought I had about four day's worth, maybe five if I ate light. My list of items wasn't very large, canned goods, more meat and potatoes than vegetables, maybe some canned spaghetti and meat balls for a change, a big canteen, some nuts to chew on while I was riding, and I decided to split the stewed tomatoes with an equal amount of canned peaches. I could be a little more selective in a grocery store than in my ex-boss's kitchen.

Satisfied that I knew where I was going, thanks to the highway patrolman, and confident that I could get enough supplies to last me a few more days, I turned in. I enjoyed laying in my bedroll, listening to the wind moving softly through the aspens, hearing the creek gurgling not too far away, and looking at the stars. It was relaxing and it generally didn't take me long to fall asleep. And I had slept good on this trip.

I was getting used to waking up with the sun, and although it was a little chilly, I really didn't mind. I enjoyed it more when I got the fire going and got some hot coffee.

I reviewed my shopping list and added a can opener and a small hand axe. My pocketknife was getting dull from cutting the tops off the cans. I decided I'd make some more selections while I was in the grocery store and maybe even splurge a little. I also decided I'd eat a meal in a café and maybe even have some ice cream and pie for dessert.

I looked over at Roman as he hobbled his way to camp. He was coming to camp every morning just to get his double handful of grain. He'd been rode every day, but was maintaining himself in good shape.

Sally was maintaining herself; she actually seemed to be gaining weight. "That would figure," I thought to myself. "Her pack is losing a little weight each day." I'd have to be careful not to get too much groceries and add even more weight. A little more grain for them might be wise.

"Ah, yes! A few apples for all of us might be good!" I halfway suspected I'd eat the apples myself, as I thought out loud. "A set of hobbles for Sally might be a good idea!" Sally had got her lead rope wrapped around some trees, thereby shortening her grazing area.

I got Roman saddled and Sally packed and started up the

road. According to the directions I'd got from the highway patrolman, there were forest service campgrounds all along this road and I shouldn't have a problem finding a place to camp with water. The day was uneventful, as they all had been.

Except for a few vehicles driving up the road to the campgrounds, I was alone.

Sally seemed to be slowing down some, trying to get extra mouthfuls of grass along the way. I'd cuss her some, jerk on her lead rope, and we'd proceed. I thought my idea of getting another set of hobbles for her and turning her loose at night was good. That way she could eat all she wanted, get water when she wanted and, more or less, be on her own.

I made camp that night in a grove of aspens, with plenty of grass and water. Supper was the same, although I was getting kinda bored with it. I gathered up plenty of firewood and turned in early that night.

I woke up early the next morning with the strange feeling that something was wrong! I couldn't quite put my finger on it!

I saw Roman, closer to camp than usual, but still close to camp. Sally was at the end of the lariat-lead rope that I'd fixed up for her. At first glance, there appeared to be nothing wrong there. I shifted my gaze around through the aspens, and then quickly looked back at Sally. There was something wrong! All of the sudden, Sally had four extra legs on her off side.

During the night, probably earlier in the morning, Sally had foaled. That's what was different. I had become the proud owner of a new baby jackass! Was it a donkey or a mule?

I remembered that my ex-boss told me she was going to foal, but didn't know what she was bred to. "Funny how we forget things, then when they happen, suddenly remember 'em," I said, as I walked around to get a look at our new addition.

Closer inspection revealed a female, a jenny colt.

"Well, hello there Little Sis," I whispered, as I slowly walked toward the jenny. "What are you doing here?"

Slowly, I patted the new arrival on the rump while she nursed. Her rump was still sticky damp, so she wasn't too old. She was still kinda shaky on her feet, just barely an hour or so old. Sally watched me curiously, but not alarmed or overly protective of her new family member. A few more pats on the rump and I decided to go build a fire and make some coffee.

While drinking the coffee, I did some thinking.

"I suppose I should rest an extra day or two, give Sally some time to gain some strength an' the new one some time to get used to being on earth and her new environment." I knew this would really slow me down; I certainly wouldn't be able to travel as fast as I had been with the new jenny. "Well, a day's rest won't hurt anything."

I surveyed the situation. There was plenty of feed for another day or two, although I would have to lead Sally to water two or three times during the day. I'd need to gather up some more firewood, but there was plenty around. I did have enough groceries, but I'd have to replenish my stock before too long. "I guess," I said to myself, "a day of rest won't hurt anything and everybody will benefit."

I had another cup of coffee and set about gathering more firewood. I hadn't given it any thought, but I'd lost track of time. I didn't know the date or even the day of the week. Thinking about a day of rest got me to thinking about what day of the week it was, and I didn't know.

The highway patrolman had told me there was a rodeo in the next town, and as I lounged around camp that day, I got to wishing I was in town. I'd have something to do while we rested, rather than just be bored in camp.

I tried to pass time by thinking up a name for the new jenny, but didn't have any luck. The colt's personality hadn't developed enough to provide me with a name.

"I suppose Little Sis will suffice for now," I said. "I can change it when the opportunity arises."

I took a little nap later on in the afternoon, although it was not fully satisfying. The shade had moved and left me in the sunlight. I woke up sweating and hot. Checking my horse and two burros, everything was all right.

My trip was going good, although the baby burro, Little Sis, was going to slow me down some. I had plenty of time. I thought maybe I should saddle Roman and ride ahead to scout the trail I was going to take, but decided not to. The day of rest would do the horse good.

I stayed in the same camp that night, although I was somewhat restless and anxious to get moving. The next day I was up early, got all the coffee I could stand, packed Sally, saddled Roman and got moving. It was good to be moving, although I set a slower pace with the new burro following closely at Sally's side.

A few miles up the road, we entered the National Forest and started to see some pretty nice campsites marked out by the forest. Some were already occupied by families planning on spending some time picnicking and camping. Occasionally, youngsters would come running out to watch us go by.

I would caution the youngsters "Don't run!"

Invariably, they would ask, "How old is the baby?"

"She was just born yesterday morning."

"Can we pet her?"

I would stop, get off my horse, get a hold of the little burro, and let the kids pet the colt, one at a time. I thought this might get the jenny used to being around people and it was sorta fun to watch the kid's expressions as they played with the new critter.

This happened quite often.

The parents would generally arrive, caution the kids and question me about what I was doing. Sometimes they would give me a couple of bucks for letting the kids pet the burro and answer their questions. I could see how this might become a profitable situation and quite often was torn between moving on and letting the kids pet Little Sis for an extended period of time in hopes of making some extra money.

The petting delays were slowing down my progress, but I was making some money. As the day passed, I started looking for a place I could camp, preferably a good distance away from other campers. I was beginning to enjoy my solitude, particularly after some lengthy visits with the campers.

I found a suitable campsite, relatively isolated from other campers and set about unpacking Sally and staking her out. There was plenty of feed and her extended lead rope had been sufficient to allow her to get enough to eat. As I was about ready to unsaddle Roman, a family camped about a hundred yards away showed up. There were four kids and Mom and Dad. The kids probably ranged in age from four or five to ten or eleven.

"Can we pet the baby?"

I was getting used to the question. "As soon as I'm done here," I replied.

I unsaddled Roman, hobbled him, gave him some grain, turned him loose and caught Little Sis so the kids could pet her. She was getting used to this and submitted to this treatment easily. As I held the colt, I got to thinking, "If this is going to be the routine, I need to get her a halter and a lead rope. That will make it easy and will halter break her at the same time. I'll get one when I get to town and get a set of hobbles for Sally at the same time."

I answered the same questions for this family as I did for the others, but was getting a little short with them. It was getting late in the day and I still had to gather up firewood and make some supper for myself. I didn't much care for the idea of gathering firewood after dark.

Presently, the Mom said, "I've got to go and start dinner."

"Yep," I said, "I've got to be doin' the same."

"Why don't you come eat with us?"

"I've got plenty here," I said.

"So do we," said Mom. "We're having fish we just caught today, trout, and there's plenty. You better come eat with us!"

Her reply sounded more like an order than a request. I started to decline again but much to my surprise, all the kids demanded that I join them for dinner.

"Well," I said, "I guess I could, but I've got some things to do around here first."

"What do you got to do around here?" The oldest boy was quite outspoken.

"Oh, I've got to set up camp, stake out Sally, gather firewood and set up camp," I said.

"We can help you do that, then you can eat with us."

"That's settled," said Mom. "Dinner will be ready in about an hour and you'll be there!" Mom left to fix supper.

"Better be there, son," said Dad, "she's set in her ways."

"Yes sir," I said. The thought of a fresh, fried trout supper was becoming more enticing. "It sure would be a nice change from stew or beans," I thought.

"You kids need to let Little Sis alone now," I said. "I think she might be wantin' to get some supper herself. I'm goin' to turn her loose an' I don't want her to kick you."

"Is that her name?" one of the little girls asked.

"For now," I replied.

"That's not a good name for her," said the youngest girl.

I asked, "How come?"

"That's what Daddy calls me and I don't want to be named after a donkey!"

Her comment brought a laugh from everybody and I think Dad enjoyed it the most.

"What would you call her?"

"I'd call her Flower," replied the girl.

"How come?"

"Because flowers are pretty and she's pretty," answered the girl.

"I don't know that any burros are pretty," I said. "Besides that, I don't want a critter named Flower. How's 'bout 'Killer'?" I said jokingly to the youngster.

"No! She's too nice for that name!"

"Then what?"

"Killer's good," said one of the boys.

"Why?"

"She tried to kick me!"

I'd been holding the colt and she hadn't really tried to kick the boy, she'd been kicking at a fly at her flanks.

"Well," I said, "let's call her Sassy if she tried to kick you. Maybe that name fits."

There seemed to be a general agreement.

"That's what it is then," I said, "Sassy!"

"I'm going to call her Flower," said the little girl.

I got the kids away and turned Sassy, or sometimes Flower, loose. I started unpacking my gear and one of the kids asked, "What do you want us to do?"

"You can gather up some firewood if you want," I answered.

The kids started immediately getting wood. Even the littlest girl was pitching in, although what she was gathering up didn't amount to much more than kindling. That was all right, I needed kindling to start the fire in the morning. By the time I had my gear unpacked and halfway settled, the kids had more firewood gathered up than I figured on using while I was there. I thought I might spend an extra day just to use up all that wood.

Before long, Mom called. Supper was ready.

Fresh fried trout, corn on the cob, taters, even a salad! I thought I was doing pretty good heating up stew in the can on an open fire, and maybe having some stewed tomatoes for dessert, but this gal really knew how to cook. And when she dished up my plate, she must have thought I was starving. Two trout, two ears of corn, two helpings of taters, all on one plate, and then she dished up a separate plate filled with salad! I wasn't sure I could eat it all. I tried to refuse so much, but she wouldn't let me, then, to top it off, she gave me a bottle of pop.

"You gave me too much food," I said. "I'll never get this all ate!"

"I'm sure you'll do all right," said Mom.

We made small talk as we ate, with me doing most of the talking. I was just answering the questions they asked, sometimes embellishing my answers, and I didn't even have much of a chance to ask them any. I found out that their name was Johnstone. I did manage to eat everything I was served and was plenty full, but managed to take another soda pop when it was offered. The youngest girl was fascinated with my spurs and kept rolling the rowels.

"Do you really use these on your horse?" she asked.

"Nope," I replied. "I just use 'em to keep me from rollin' out of bed at night."

"Make sure you save some room for ice cream!" Mom was certainly looking out for my welfare. But I wasn't sure I had room for anything else. While Mom was dishing up ice cream, I did have a chance to ask a question.

"Ice cream!" I was amazed. "How do you keep it from melting?"

"We've got a refrigerator in the motor home and a generator. Keeps everything really cold," answered Dad.

These folks really knew how to go camping.

"Where are you folks from?"

"Brooklyn, New York," answered Dad.

"That's a long way from home," I said. "How'd you get here? What'd you do, get on the wrong road?"

"This is our vacation," answered Dad. "The kids wanted to see the real Wild West. You're about the closest thing we've come to it yet."

"There ain't too much wild about me," I said. I thought that maybe I should exaggerate my answers to their questions a little more and give them a taste of a really Wild West.

We visited quite late into the night, but I was content to let my supper settle and sit and visit. I hadn't ate that much for a long time. I finally managed to get away and stumble back to my camp and hit the sack.

The Johnstone's were a nice family and the kids talked a lot. I ended up finding out more information than I needed or wanted to know.

I slept good that night and even slept in a little the next morning. I got up, made a fire, and got some coffee started. My new-found friends from the night before weren't up yet, I guess they'd stayed up too late the night before, too.

The coffee was just coming to a boil when Dad came out of the motor home and started walking toward my camp.

I decided to meet him half way.

"Get a cup an' have some coffee by the fire," I said, as he approached. "I only got one cup. This coffee's pretty strong; you might want to bring some cream an' sugar."

Dad abruptly turned around and went back to the motor home. He emerged with a cup, a carton of half and half, and a bowl of sugar.

"Just help yourself," I said, as he approached the fire. "It's ready."

"I hope the kids didn't bother you too much last night," he said, as he settled down on the ground. "You sure captivated them. Are you sure everything you told them is true?"

"Well, not exactly," I said, grinning. "I did have a good time compounding my story."

"You know, I kinda envy you."

"Oh really? How come?" I was surprised someone would envy *me*.

"You're young, don't seem to have any cares and are doing just what you want to. You've really got the best thing going for you right now."

"I don't know about that," I said. "I do have to get home in time for school, get school clothes an' all that stuff. By the way, what day is it today?"

Dad looked at his watch. "It's seven-ten in the morning, July twenty-fourth. And it's Thursday."

35

I'd completely lost track of time. I did some quick figuring; I still had enough time to make it home in time for school. But I'd have to keep moving at a pretty steady pace. Sally and Sassy would slow me down, but I'd have to keep moving.

Thought of moving down the highway, with Sally loaded down with newly purchased groceries in town, and Sassy tagging along brought a smile to my face. I visualized the picture in my mind … we more than resembled a gypsy outfit.

"I better be moving along," I said, as I got up. "I've still got a lot of ground to cover an' I've got to get some groceries when I get to town."

I was hoping to get moving before the kids came out and started pestering me with questions.

"Well son," said Dad, "you take care of yourself."

He stuck out his hand to say goodbye and I took it. When he let go, I found a fifty-dollar bill in my hand. I had the fleeting thought that maybe my outfit looked more like beggars than gypsies.

"I don't need this," I protested, as I went to give it back to him.

"Yes you do," said Dad. "You keep it; you never know when you might need it. Maybe we'll see you at the rodeo in town day after tomorrow. You'll need some money to get in to see it."

"Day after tomorrow? I won't need any money to get in, but I will need some money for entry fees," I said.

"Just keep it," said Dad, as he walked back to camp.

I gathered up Roman and Sally, gave them each some grain and went to packing my gear. It didn't take long to get packed and ready to start out. As I climbed into the saddle, the kids came out of the motor home.

It seemed like they didn't want me to leave, but I'm sure their fascination with Sassy was a more prevailing factor.

"We've got to get going, kids. We might see you in town at the rodeo. Your Dad said you were going to watch it."

"He said you were going to be in it!"

"Yep! I better get going."

I touched a spur to Roman, hollered at Sally and started to move out. I was finally on the way.

Traveling was uneventful. I spent a lot of time enjoying the scenery, but the scenery doesn't change much when a person is moving by horseback.

As the day wore on, I began looking for a place to camp, preferably a little farther from other campers than the night before.

I really did enjoy that meal the night before. My own cooked supper of stew didn't seem quite as nice and I resolved to vary my menu a lot more at the grocery store. I slept real good that night and was up early the next morning. Another day's riding I figured would put me in town.

Rodeo

The ride down the mountain was fairly steep and I could see where a vehicle might have a tough time of it in some spots. But Roman handled it and Sally didn't have any problems. Sassy seemed to have a hard time adjusting to the slope, but finally figured it out.

The road leveled out and widened and soon it became paved. I found the fairgrounds and the groundskeeper.

"You made it just in time," said the groundskeeper. "I was just fixing to leave for the night. Big day tomorrow, what with the rodeo and everything going on."

I made arrangements to rent a couple of pens overnight and get some feed for my stock. The pens were under a pavilion, about fifteen feet by fifteen feet. There were water troughs in each pen. I even got a pen for myself to camp in.

"How far is it into town?" I asked the groundskeeper. I was a little concerned about taking my outfit into town. It would certainly raise some curiosity, and I was sure the grocery store didn't have a hitch rack to tie Roman and Sally to while I did my shopping.

"It's only about a half mile to the general store from here. Another half mile to the café," he answered. "If you're looking to get to the café, I can give you a ride, I'm about done here."

"I'd appreciate a ride to the café after I get unpacked an' unsaddled," I said.

"You got it," he replied.

"Where do you get signed up for the rodeo?"

"You figuring on entering?"

"Yep," I said.

"The entries are at the café."

"Good. I can kill two birds with one stone."

The special in the café was stew. That didn't really appeal to me since I'd had plenty on this trip and sorta figured I'd be having some more. I finally settled on fried chicken. I hadn't had that for a long time. A root beer float topped off the meal. I really felt like I was living like a king.

As I paid my bill, I entered the bareback bronc riding. It cost me twenty dollars, but I really figured on winning some money.

As I walked back to the fairgrounds, I passed the general store. This was a real old-time store with groceries, hardware, some tack items, just a little bit of everything. I resolved to do all my shopping there in the morning, before the rodeo started.

Before I hit the sack, I reviewed my shopping list. I'd added a halter for Sassy and a set of hobbles for Sally to the list. I also added another lead rope for Sassy. I circled the axe and can opener and toilet paper. I sure didn't want to overlook these items. I went to bed planning on doing my shopping in the morning, riding in the bareback bronc riding in the afternoon, and pulling out the next day.

I felt a little strange sleeping under the pavilion and not being able to look at the stars, and some of the other contestants made some noise pulling in late and unloading their horses, but I managed to sleep fairly well.

I was up early the next morning and looking for a cup of coffee, but couldn't build a fire at the fairgrounds. I fed Roman and Sally. I was sure the general store wasn't open yet, but the café should be. I didn't much like the idea of walking into town, but figured I could get all the coffee I wanted at the café while I was waiting for the general store to open.

There were some other people in the café, mostly farm and ranch people, just starting the day. With the rodeo and the county fair being held at the same time, the little town had taken on a holiday atmosphere. There didn't seem to be any rush to get started with anything. I lingered with my coffee, making sure I gave the general store plenty of time to open up. Making sure I had my list, once I got my fill of coffee, I went to the general store.

The first things I bought were the hobbles, a new halter and lead rope for Sassy, a fifty-pound sack of grain, then I started looking for my own groceries, including a can opener. I had quite a pile of goods when I was finished. The store clerk smiled as I paid him.

"How you going to get all this where you want it?"

Kind of embarrassed, I answered, "I don't know." I hadn't given any thought to carrying it all back to the fairgrounds, and it amounted to quite a bit. It might take a couple of trips.

"I saw you walking into town this morning on my way to work. And I heard about you from my brother-in-law."

I asked, "Who's your brother-in-law?"

"He's the highway patrolman that stopped you on the highway a few days ago. He seemed kinda concerned about you."

"Does that mean I'm famous?"

"I don't know about that," he answered, "but there has been

quite a bit of talk about you. I know how you're traveling. If you want, you can leave all this stuff in the back room, then bring your horse and burro to the back door and pick it up."

"But I ain't figurin' on leavin' 'till tomorrow." I thought I'd spend another day.

"It'll be all right," replied the clerk.

I stored the stuff in the back room, but took the halter and lead rope back to the fairgrounds with me. I thought it might be a good idea to tie Sassy to Sally while we went through town.

I didn't have anything to do before the rodeo started, so I wandered through the midway at the fairgrounds after leaving the halter and lead rope in the pen where I was sleeping. I wasn't much interested in going on any of the rides or trying to win any of the cheap prizes, but it was interesting to watch the other people having their fun.

The rodeo was slated to start at one o'clock and the bareback bronc riding was the first event after the grand entry. As rodeo time approached, I made my way to the bucking chutes to look over the stock. Behind the chutes, I found my name as a contestant and the number of the horse I had drawn, 03.

I was disappointed in 03. He was small, not much bigger than a Welsh pony, and a paint—sorrel and white. His size probably meant he was fast and quick.

"Well," I thought, "maybe I can make some money on him."

I went to look for the stock contractor to see of I could borrow a bareback rigging and maybe find out what the little paint horse did when they opened the gate. I managed to find the stock contractor and make arrangements to borrow rigging.

I asked, "What's he do?"

"He bucks," replied the contractor. The answer was curt— short and to the point.

"Any particular pattern or rhythm?"

"Nope," came the reply. "He's fast an' pretty smart. He's been around, knows all the tricks; he's a pretty wise ol' codger. He's bucked off a lot of good cowboys! If you can ride him, you'll be in the money."

"Thanks," I said, and left. I wandered back through the midway, just killing time waiting for rodeo time and met the Johnstone family. They seemed excited to see me. I was immediately surrounded by the family and showered with more questions.

"Are you all right? Are you eating well? Are you entered in the rodeo? In what event? How's Flower?"

There were so many questions, coming so fast, I didn't have a chance to answer any of them. I finally said, "Yes, I'm entered in the bareback bronc ridin'. It's just about ready to start an' I got to get goin'. Flower's fine."

I was wanting to get away. While the Johnstone's were nice, I was sorta overwhelmed by them, and it was getting close to rodeo time.

I went back behind the chutes, more to hide than anything else. The bareback broncs were in the chutes, and I put my borrowed rigging on 03. He was peaceful in the chute and the excitement was starting to build in me.

The grand entry had finished, introductions made, and the bareback bronc riding had started. The way things were going, it looked like I'd be the fifth rider out.

I watched the other bronc riders. One feller bucked off, a couple of others made their rides, although their scores weren't impressive, and then the fourth rider had trouble with his horse in the chute.

"Next rider get ready!" It was the chute boss.

I was the next rider. I settled down on 03 gingerly, got my

hand hold, got my feet in position, leaned back, and asked for the gate.

The little horse didn't hesitate when the gate opened. He came straight up, pushing me back a little. I stretched my feet as far forward as I could, trying to make sure I marked the horse out. If I didn't have my feet in the proper position when the horse took his first jump, I wouldn't get a score and wouldn't make any money. I'd been in a few bareback bronc riding contests before.

The horse hit the ground hard on the first jump, pushing me foreword. I immediately leaned back, and started spurring, from the point of the horse's shoulder as high up his neck as I could.

The horse's second jump seemed higher than the first, and I continued to spur as fast and as high as I could. When he hit the ground the second time, I was loosened a little and realized I was not in time with him. I leaned back as far as I could and tried to get some rhythm with the horse.

His next jump was as high as the others and on this one he twisted to the left. That loosened me a little more and I felt myself tilting to the right. The thought went through my mind, "How can such a little horse be so stout?"

I was out of time with the horse and struggling to get back to the proper balance on him. I could hear the crowd yelling. Briefly I saw myself righted on the horse and making a good ride.

The next jump was to the left again and I felt myself loosened a little more. With all the strength I had, I pulled myself back to the center of the horse. Then with the next jump, the little horse went back to the right and I started sliding off to the left. I was still leaning back as far as I could, trying to spur as much as I could, but I had my hands full just trying to stay on.

43

The next jump, the horse went back to the left, and I got square with the horse. 03 had bucked back under me, and I managed to regain the proper position. Then, the horse just bucked in place, he stayed in one place and just jumped as high in the air as he could. When he hit the ground, he hit it hard, and started to loosen me again.

I was beginning to think that my eight-second ride should be about up and began wondering why I hadn't heard the whistle. All of a sudden, the little horse made a big jump to the left, and I started to slide to the right. I could feel my grip on the rigging loosening as I slid to the right. I hit the ground with my right hand first, then my right shoulder.

I felt a sharp pain in my right wrist then a pain in my shoulder. Right before I hit the ground, I heard the whistle.

In my mind I had made a qualified ride, but the announcer was saying, "And all that cowboy gets today is a round of applause from you folks!"

I got up, holding my wrist. I was hoping I hadn't broke it. I went to the judge.

"I think I was still on the horse when the whistle blew," I said. In my mind I thought I had made one heck of a ride and stood a good chance of winning it all.

"I'll give you that," said the judge, "an' you did make a real good ride, but you missed him out."

"I'm sure I marked him out," I said.

"No," said the judge. "On that first jump out of the chute, you slid back an' didn't have your spurs over the point of the horse's shoulder. I had to goose-egg you."

There wasn't much sense in arguing with the judge, he'd flagged me right at the beginning. My efforts and my money were wasted.

I walked over to the ambulance, still holding my wrist. If it was broken, I'd need to get it set.

The ambulance attendant was cordial. "That was a good ride you made on that little horse."

"Not good enough," I said. "They said I missed him out. But I kinda hurt my wrist when I landed."

"Let me see."

I stuck out my wrist. It was starting to swell, and it still hurt.

"Looks like it's broke to me," said the attendant. "We better take you in and have a doctor look at it. But I can't leave here unless they stop the show. I'll call and maybe someone else can run you in."

The attendant made a call on his radio. "They're sending someone to take you in. Just wait here, they'll be here shortly."

While I was waiting for my ride, the Johnstone family showed up.

"A very good ride you made, my boy!" Dad Johnstone was sounding very proper. "Did you hurt yourself?"

"I didn't hurt myself," I replied. "But I did get hurt."

"Are you all right?" The youngest girl was concerned. Then she asked, "How's Flower?"

"Flower's fine," I answered. "I think I busted my wrist. I'll have to go to the doc's an' find out."

"Anything we can do to help?" The dad was genuinely concerned.

"If I don't make it back before dark, make sure Roman, Sally, and Sassy are fed. I'd ..."

"You mean Flower," interrupted the little girl.

"I'd sure appreciate it," I said, ignoring her.

I was becoming a little agitated. I'd made what I thought was a good ride, only to find out I didn't. I'd lost my entry fees. I had what I thought was a broken wrist and this little girl wanted to correct me on the name of my baby burro! I was not in a good mood.

Presently, the sheriff showed up.

"I'm taking you in," he said, as he approached.

"To jail?"

The sheriff laughed. "No, to the doc's."

"We'll take care of your animals," said Dad Johnstone, as the sheriff and I left.

On the way to the hospital, the sheriff was just as curious as the highway patrolman had been earlier. I had to repeat the story about going home the way I was because I didn't have a truck to haul my animals.

At the hospital, the doctor looked at my wrist, did some poking around with the usual "Hums" and "Haas" that doctors generally say when making an examination. I never have figured out the sense behind these one-sided conversations.

Finally, he volunteered, "I don't think it's broken, probably just a bad sprain. But we'll take some x-rays just to make sure."

The x-rays didn't show anything broken, but the wrist was swollen, making movement difficult and painful. I didn't say anything about my shoulder since the pain was going away.

"Just a bad sprain," said the Doc. "Don't use it for a couple of days and it will be all right. I can bandage it to keep it stable so you can't move it. You can make arrangements to pay at the front desk."

The doctor bandaged my wrist with an Ace Wrap bandage. I thought it was quite extensive, and it did immobilize my wrist. I thought he was going to great lengths and was about to say something about "it wasn't necessary to gift wrap that, Christmas is a long ways away," but decided to keep quiet. A lot of these adults weren't paying much attention to me anyway.

I was surprised to see the sheriff waiting for me at the receptionist's desk.

"I don't guess you broke it, kid. There's not a cast on it."

"Just sprained bad," I said. "What are you doin' here?"

"Thought I'd stick around and give you a ride back to the rodeo grounds."

I paid the doctor bill. It occurred to me that I hadn't counted my money and had no idea how much I had left. I resolved to count my funds later that night before I went to bed.

I asked the sheriff to drive me around to the pavilion where I had my stock housed. I was surprised to see that the gates to both my pens were open and my horse and burros were gone! My saddle was also missing!

"Sheriff, my horse an' burros have been stolen!"

"Oh, those folks that fed them probably just left the gate open."

"My saddle is gone, too! My whole outfit has been stolen!"

The sheriff made a quick look around then went to his patrol car and made a call.

"I put out an all points bulletin regarding your horse and burros. They can't be hard to see, there aren't that many burros in the county. We should have them back shortly."

The sheriff's words were meant to console me, but it wasn't working. I became very concerned about my livestock—where they were and how I was going to get them back. I couldn't relax, just about everything I owned was gone, the whole summer's work.

"You stick around here and see if you can spot your animals. I'll patrol around, ask some questions and see what I can find out. Somebody may have seen them leave." The sheriff was pretty firm in his directions.

"I'd just as soon go with you," I said. "If we find 'em, I can identify 'em for you."

"Okay," the sheriff said. "Get in."

After questioning some folks, the sheriff did find someone that had seen the horse and burros leaving the fairgrounds in the back of a red pickup truck with a stock rack. They told us that the truck had turned north on the main road and that there were two guys in the truck, drinking.

The sheriff got on the radio again and said something about "the suspects are in a red pickup, with a horse and two burros in the rear headed north."

Presently a call came over the radio from a highway patrolman. He had the "suspects" pulled over up the highway a piece and was requesting assistance. The sheriff turned on his siren and we sped up the road. I don't think I'd ever gone so fast in my life.

When we arrived at the scene where the highway patrolman had the "suspects" pulled over, he had one "suspect" handcuffed to the stock rack and the other spread-eagle on the ground.

"Hello Hal." The sheriff appeared to know everyone in the county.

"Hello Bert. You got the kid with you. What kinda trouble is he in now?"

The highway patrolman was the same one that had pulled me over on the highway earlier.

"He's not in trouble. But his horse and burros turned up missing. Looks like you found them."

"I thought they looked familiar, but I didn't pull them over for that. These guys were weaving pretty bad down the road, I figured they were drunk. The one on the ground couldn't pass the sobriety test. Your call came over the radio after I had them pulled over. Looks like the kid added a member to his bunch."

"They stole my horse an' burros," I said.

"We didn't steal nothin'," said the man handcuffed to the truck.

"How'd they come to be in the truck?" The sheriff's mood had changed from cordial to very stern and businesslike.

"We just found 'em wandering down the road an' put 'em in the truck to take 'em to their rightful owner." The speech of the man handcuffed to the truck was slurred.

"That's right sheriff," said the man on the ground.

"You just be quiet," the highway patrolman said.

"If you just found them, how'd that saddle get on the horse? I been ridin' that horse all summer, an' not once has he saddled himself in the morning!" I was relieved to have my horse and burros back, but mad that they had been stolen. "There's a law about horse stealin' in this state, ain't there? Somethin' about hangin'," I continued. I was pretty brave when I had the sheriff on my side.

"You be quiet, too," the sheriff told me. "You'll get your chance."

"Tell that kid to shut up," said the man handcuffed to the truck.

"You be quiet, too," said the sheriff. "There's entirely too much talk goin' on here and nobody's saying anything!"

The highway patrolman went to his car and made a call on his radio.

"I've got some help coming to drive the truck in. These guys are too drunk to drive. We'll transport them to jail and let them sober up overnight. We might hold them longer while the kid presses charges."

"How long will that take?" I was concerned about getting moving and I knew it would be slower with Sassy. "I don't want

49

to spend all summer here waiting for a trial. I'm content to get my livestock back."

Presently another highway patrolman and a sheriff's deputy showed up. The sheriff told his deputy to drive the pickup back to the fairgrounds, unload the horse and burros and take the truck to the impound lot. He also told the deputy to take me with him so I could take proper care of the animals at the fairgrounds. He and the other officers would transport the "suspects" to jail.

The ride back to the fairgrounds was uneventful, although it seemed to me that it took considerably longer than the ride out with the sheriff. Of course that ride had been at top speed with the siren going. Once again, I had to repeat my story to the cop driving me back to the fairgrounds.

The rodeo was about over when we reached the fairgrounds, and a lot of the contestants were leaving. The spectators would stick around and do the rides and games on the midway.

I found the groundskeeper and made arrangements to stay over another night.

"You've had a pretty rough day," he said. "You go ahead and stay in the pens you used last night. I won't charge you."

I was kinda surprised that everyone seemed to know what was happening before I did, but I'm told news travels fast in a small town.

I thanked the groundskeeper and told him I'd be leaving in the morning, after the general store opened.

I didn't have to feed that night; the Johnstone's had put plenty of feed out.

Sleep was restless that night—my wrist was hurting and my shoulder had a dull ache that made it painful to lie on.

I was up fairly early the next morning, looking to get saddled, get my new supplies, get some coffee at the café, and get going.

I had a hard time throwing my saddle on Roman and ended up laying the cinches and right stirrup over the seat and just placing the saddle on him. My well-wrapped wrist was hindering my actions and I didn't have full use or strength of it. But I got it done.

Sally was easier to saddle—she was much smaller than Roman.

I couldn't put my chaps on, I couldn't get them buckled in the back with my wrist wrapped the way it was. I just looped my chaps over the saddle horn and figured that would work.

"It'll probably be cooler," I thought. "There ain't much use for 'em ridin' out in the open."

I put the halter on Sassy, tied her lead rope to Sally's saddle, got on Roman and headed out.

It was hard to get on my horse—my wrist was hurting me and there wasn't any strength in it. I grinned as I thought of me walking away, leading my animals rather than riding, and the thought of looking more like gypsies than anything else entered my mind. I thought I had better find a rock or a log to stand on to help me get on until my wrist got better.

Sassy was reluctant to move, but with her being tied to Sally, she didn't have much choice. I thought she'd be well halter broken by the end of her first day being led. Her head might be a little sore, but if that were the case, she'd have an easier time of it in the future.

I got to the café, tied my animals out in the back and went inside to get my coffee. Carelessly, I hadn't given any thought to getting back on Roman as I got off. I drank a little more coffee than I needed, putting off having to get back on.

I got to the general store and got my supplies packed in the panniers, as even in weight as I could get them. As small as Sally was, I still had a tough time getting the loaded panniers on the pack saddle. The store clerk gave me a hand. I was grateful for that, and wondered how tough it would be when I'd be alone the next morning.

I got some fairly sketchy directions from the clerk as we loaded my supplies, on how to get out of town and find a peaceful route to my destination.

I put the sack of grain in the middle of the load, on top of my bedroll, tied it down with a lash rope and headed out.

As I left, the store clerk hollered, "Here," and tossed a can of pop to me.

I caught it, said, "Thanks," and started out. About ten yards away from the back door of the store, I decided to open the pop because I was having a hard time handling the reins in my left hand and Sally's lead rope along with the pop in my right hand, with it being bandaged like it was.

As soon as I popped the top on the pop, it fizzed and shot out of the can. Roman shied to the left and I almost fell off! I dropped the pop, but held onto the lead rope and managed to get Roman under control.

"Do you want another one?" The store clerk was grinning. "We've got plenty!"

"I don't think so," I replied. "I can't even handle what I had." I was grinning at the situation myself. I imagined it made a fairly humorous picture.

Heading out, I was somewhat relieved to be leaving civilization. I had experienced a fairly exhausting weekend.

Out of town, I stayed on a dirt road for a few miles until I got to the forest. I was relieved to be riding in the forest. The dirt road had been out in the open and it was starting to get hot. At least there was some shade in the forest.

I always liked riding in the trees. It was cooler and a feller always stood the chance of seeing some wildlife, shaded up during the day.

I hadn't seen much wildlife on this trip. I'd seen some deer along the way; the bucks were in velvet still, growing some antlers. The fawns were just starting to lose their spots. I thought some of the bigger bucks would have some big racks and make someone a nice trophy during the deer hunt.

The first day out from the rodeo, I made camp early. Sally, reaching down to grab some grass, had been jerking on my wrist. I finally made a loop in the end of her lead rope and just looped it around my saddle horn. This relieved the pain in my wrist some, but the wrist was still painful, hence my decision to make camp early. I found a spot in the forest with feed and water and made camp. Making camp was not for the benefit of my animals, but for the benefit of my wrist.

I did have some difficulty unloading my panniers and unsaddling my horse, but got it done. I sure wasn't as fast as I had been as I set about making my camp. I hobbled Sally with her new hobbles, gave her some grain and turned her loose. I didn't think she'd wander off very far.

I was anxious to try out my new hand axe, but couldn't really use my right hand. The axe was sharp and even with my left hand, getting firewood was easier. However, I am not a left-handed axe man, and almost hit myself in the left leg. I resolved to be more careful with the axe. I was already about half-crippled, I didn't need to complete the job!

I hit the sack early that night and slept a little better. I was up early the next morning, but didn't get in a big rush about getting moving. I did get the coffee going. My wrist didn't seem to be feeling any better and it was hard for me to get motivated. Plus my shoulder was still bothering me.

I finally finished with the coffee, got Roman saddled, threw my chaps over the saddle horn, saddled Sally and got the panniers on and the rest of my gear packed. I caught Sassy and led her over to Sally and tied her to the pack saddle. Her being pulled by Sally the day before had pretty well taught her to lead and I didn't have the problem I'd anticipated.

Getting on Roman was still a chore, but I found a fallen tree to give me a little help. We started out without any problems, and I made a mental note to make camp where there was a tree stump or rock I could use to help me get mounted.

As we moved on, I noticed a big bank of clouds developing in the western sky.

"We might get a little rain later," I said to Roman. "It won't hurt the country, the grass is startin' to dry up. Might make it taste a little better for you, Old Man."

The clouds were building up fast and began to look threatening. I double-checked my saddle—my rain slicker was still tied behind the seat. I hadn't really paid attention to it, I just always kept it there. I hadn't used it all summer, but it was something that was mighty handy to have when it was needed.

"I hope it hasn't dry-rotted during the summer," I said, as I looked behind the cantle, double-checking.

Watching the clouds build, I decided to get off and get my denim jacket out of one of my panniers. I thought it might get a little chilly with a rainstorm. I started looking for a place where I could make it easier to get back on. Getting on was becoming easier, but only with the help of something to stand on. It was still awkward and difficult, but becoming manageable.

It was only about fifteen or twenty minutes later when the wind picked up and the rain started. I put on my rain slicker and none too soon. I also halfway put on my chaps, although I still couldn't get them buckled in the back due to my wrist.

The rain soon turned to sleet and it came down hard, and then turned to hail. The hail was about the size of a marble, and it hurt a little when it hit. I was having a hard time keeping Roman under control. He was responding to the slightly punishing pounding of the hail. Sally was resolved to endure the punishment and Sassy was completely baffled by this quirk of nature. She didn't know what to do and consequently struggled and jumped around. I was glad she was tied securely to Sally.

The animals wanted to turn tail to the storm. It had approached us from the left side and it was a constant struggle to keep Roman headed generally north. Sally also wanted to turn tail to the storm, and she kept jerking to the right to get away from the hail. I had long since given up on trying to jerk her into line, having looped her lead rope to my saddle horn. This eased the pain in my right wrist, which was still bandaged and getting wet.

I decided I'd remove the bandage when I made camp that night. I wasn't really enjoying the loss of use of my right hand.

The hail soon changed back to rain and I thought it would settle in for the night, but its intensity soon dwindled to a steady slow, soaking kind of rain. Within an hour it had stopped, and the sun was trying to come out.

Wet, and trying to warm up some, I decided to make camp early. I knew it would be difficult to find dry firewood, and I didn't particularly like the thought of making a cold camp.

I found a suitable place to make camp in a grove of aspen and pine trees. "This forest is mixed up a little," I told Sally, as I unpacked her.

Most forests have a pretty regular line of demarcation where the aspens are separated from the pines and other brush. In this area there appeared to be a struggle between the various types of vegetation to achieve dominance. This was a gift to me—it made it easier to find suitable firewood. I could get some small stuff to use as kindling from under the brush, the aspen limbs would provide some fast, hot flames, and the pine would burn longer. It was difficult to use the axe with my injured wrist but I managed to get enough gathered up to cook some supper and have enough left over to start a fire in the morning.

After I cooked supper—stew again because it was the easiest to get with my bandaged wrist—I unwrapped my wrist. I could flex it some, but it was still painful. I saved the bandage. I didn't have a use for it, but I thought it might come in handy in the future. If I didn't have a use for it, I figured I could use it to start a fire if I couldn't find any dry firewood in case I got caught in another rainstorm.

As I unrolled my bedroll, I was thankful I'd invested in a canvas bedroll tarp. My bedding was dry, but the tarp was pretty wet. I built the fire up and hit the sack. I thought that with the rainstorm and perhaps another one coming, it might get kinda cold at night.

Another Surprise

The next couple of days were pretty much alike; cool in the early mornings, warming up toward mid-morning, then an afternoon thundershower that lasted about half an hour and it would warm up before the sun went down. It made for some right nice riding.

A few days after the first rainstorm, I came across some irrigated pastures. These pastures were irrigated with sprinkler pipe. I thought there might be some pretty big money behind these ranch operations, as sprinkler pipe was expensive. I decided to stick to the mountains and stay away from these ranches. I might have to ride a few extra miles, but I wouldn't have to spend a lot of time opening gates and maybe getting into trouble for trespassing. I thought it might be nice to talk to someone and get a better idea of how to get to where I wanted to go, but I didn't want to get into trouble being on property I didn't have any business being on.

I made camp that night within sight of the irrigated pastures, but far enough away as to not be any bother to the place. I kinda felt like a criminal, not wanting to be discovered, yet needing to stay pretty close to the direction I had mapped out in my mind. Satisfied that my camp wouldn't bother anything, I cooked supper and turned in for the night, confident that if I was discovered, I wouldn't be in too much trouble.

I was awakened the next morning by the sound of gunfire and Sally making a big racket. Her braying was enough to wake up anybody, but the gunfire was different. "Somebody's shooting my burro! I've been discovered!" My thoughts were racing as I got up and pulled on my pants and boots. "Why would someone shoot my burro?"

My next thought was of the two drunks that had stole Roman, Sally, and Sassy, trying to get back at me. But I was quite a few days away from the town where that incident had occurred.

I rushed toward the sound of Sally's braying. I got to where I could see her, still hobbled, kicking at a mountain lion that was trying to get to Sassy. Sassy was confused, but trying to keep her mom between her and the lion.

"Get out of here," I hollered, as I grabbed a limb off the ground and ran to the scene. "You leave my livestock alone!"

I stopped at the sound of another rifle shot and the sight of dust being stirred up at the feet of the lion. Someone was trying to shoot the lion!

Another shot, and dust right under the nose of the lion turned him and a shot immediately following that one put the lion on the run, abandoning his intended meal. I looked to where the shots had come from and saw a man on foot carrying a rifle, walking slowly down the hill.

My thoughts turned to my livestock. Sally and Sassy appeared to be all right, but where was Roman? Surely the lion hadn't gotten him. Thoughts of having to complete my trip on foot entered my mind, and they weren't good thoughts.

The man with the rifle approached me. "Those your jack-asses?"

"Yep," I answered. "I sure do appreciate your running off the mountain lion."

"Yeah," said the man. "You couldn't have done much with that limb you're carrying."

Instinctively, I dropped the limb.

"That ain't much of a weapon against a lion. He could have got you an' the jackasses."

I realized how foolish I looked trying to fight off a mountain lion with the limb of an aspen tree. Trying to divert the topic of conversation to a less embarrassing subject, I asked him, "You seen my horse? I hobbled him last night an' he ain't come into camp yet."

"He's up on the hill," said the man, casting his arm in the direction he had come from.

I looked up the hill and saw Roman peacefully grazing, seemingly unaffected by the morning's events.

"How'd you come to be here at just the right time?" I was unaware that anyone was in the area.

"I have a herd of sheep over the hill. That lion has been bothering them for a few days. I aim to get him." The sheepherder seemed to be full of resolve.

"Don't you need dogs to hunt mountain lions?"

"My dogs are not lion dogs, they're sheepherding dogs. They'll fight off a mountain lion if he tries to attack the sheep, but they won't go out and hunt the lions."

"Where are they?"

"They're watching the sheep, just like they're supposed to." The voice of the sheepherder had taken on an ironical tone and I was becoming somewhat embarrassed again.

"What are you doin' out here?" he asked.

I seemed to create a lot of curiosity when I ran into other people. I retold my story, shortening it up considerably. When I finished, he asked, "Where's your camp?"

I pointed in the general direction of where my bedroll was laid out, but couldn't see much. I hadn't even had time to start a fire and get some coffee going.

"I've got some coffee, if you want some. It won't take long to get a fire goin' an' get some ready. You're sure welcome to join me if you like. It's the least I can do for saving my burros."

"Naw," replied the man. "You gather up your stuff an' come to my camp. By the time you get there, I'll have coffee an' something to eat fixed up." With that, he turned and walked back to where he had come from without another word.

The invitation sounded more like an order than a request, but I accepted. I had the strange idea that this sheepherder was more used to giving orders than he was in taking them.

I went back to my camp, grabbed Roman and Sally's halters and caught up my livestock. When I caught Sally and Sassy, I very carefully looked them over, making sure the lion hadn't done them any harm. They appeared to be all right and I led them back to camp.

I got them saddled and loaded without too much trouble. I didn't tie Sassy to Sally because Sassy was sticking pretty close to Sally after the morning's incident.

I was thinking it was strange that my horse and burro had strayed so far away from camp, but concluded the arrival of the mountain lion had disrupted our normal routine. I also got to thinking, "Why hadn't I brought a gun along?"

Of course I didn't have one and I really hadn't anticipated the thought of any predators approaching. I laughed at all the things that I should have brought but forgot, from toilet paper to a rifle. "Well," I thought, "I've done pretty good so far without all the things I forgot or didn't even think about. Maybe I ain't as bad off as I appear to be."

I rode over the hill and immediately spied the sheep camp. Off in the distance, I saw the sheep herd. There were a lot of them, and I could understand why they weren't close to camp. There were two horses hobbled near camp and a flatbed wagon loaded with hay. Smoke was coming from the sheepherder's wagon.

"Coffee will be ready," I thought, as I approached the camp.

The sheepherder stuck his head out the door. "Coffee's ready. Hobble your horses … that is, horse an' burro, an come an' get some. Breakfast is ready if you like your eggs well done."

I hadn't given any thought to breakfast. All summer long my breakfast consisted of coffee and coffee alone.

I hobbled my animals and approached the sheep wagon.

"Come on in. You can sit there," the man said, pointing to the bench near the table. There was already a plate full of fried potatoes, hard fried eggs, and bacon on the table. I took a seat and started to object to breakfast, but wasn't allowed to.

"You eat breakfast, it's the most important meal of the day!"

I'd heard that before, it was strangely familiar. As a matter of fact, it sounded a lot like my own mother. This sheepherder was very controlling.

I started to look for another plate, so as I could take a little and appease the herder, but was abruptly stopped.

"That's yours. All of it."

"That's more than I need," I said.

"You look like you need more than that. Eat it."

Once again, I was being commanded. I didn't think I was starving, although it had been since I ate with the Johnstone's or maybe the meal in town that I had really felt full. But I was surviving and really enjoying my trip.

I was running into a lot of controlling people—my ex-boss, the highway patrolman, the sheriff, the Johnstone dad and now this sheepherder. I was really beginning to enjoy the solitude I found on the trail. After all, Roman and Sally and Sassy didn't talk back, didn't ask questions, and didn't give orders! Yes there was some peace, contentment, and quiet in my solitude.

Trying to make small talk while we were eating, I asked, "How long you been out here with these sheep?"

"Quite a while, it seems like. I'm not really a sheepherder, I own this flock. There's more than a thousand sheep out there, more than one man can handle. But my sheepherders quit an' I don't have anybody to look after 'em. Just me an' the dogs. You lookin' for a job?"

"No," I answered. "As I said earlier, I'm headed home an' have to be there before school starts. I still got some travelin' to do."

"Looks like to me your horse could stand a rest."

I looked out the door at Roman. He had lost a little weight, but he certainly wasn't hurting.

"He's okay," I replied.

I was surprised I was offered a job. This man hadn't even asked if I was looking for work, if I had any experience or was even qualified. He must have needed help pretty bad.

"You better rest your horse a day. You can camp here tonight. Unsaddle your horse, unpack your jackass, an' turn 'em loose. We'll go check the sheep an' you can use my other horse."

I was being ordered again and I half way suspected this sheep rancher was going to take the time and try and convince me that I should go to work for him. I really wasn't interested in herding sheep.

I unsaddled Roman, unpacked Sally, hobbled them and turned them loose. The rancher had caught up his horses and was leading them to camp.

"Here, you can ride this one," he said, handing me the lead rope on a black horse.

"Anything I should know about this horse?" I was leery of riding strange horses offered to me by strangers.

"No. He's plumb gentle."

I saddled the horse and climbed up. The horse was a little taller than Roman, and I was reminded that my wrist still hurt some when I got on. Once in the saddle, I watched the rancher with his horse.

The horse was standing as if to start a fight when the rancher threw on his saddle.

I asked, "That horse of yours broke?"

I noticed the horse had a hump in his back.

"Yep. He's just a little nervous on the ground."

The rancher pulled the cinch tight and the horse went straight up in the air. His feet were about four feet off the ground. My horse shied a little at the commotion, but nothing serious.

The rancher's horse came down and stood shaking. He blew the rollers in his nose and flinched a little as the rancher patted him on the neck.

"Easy boy, easy." The rancher's tone was gentle and soothing as he talked to the horse, not commanding and gruff like when he talked to me.

He took off the hobbles and started to lead the horse around in circles, still talking in the soothing tone. "Always got to untrack a cold-backed horse before you get on," he said.

I didn't know if he was talking to me, the horse, or himself.

After walking the horse around for a minute or two, the

rancher put a foot into the stirrup and eased himself into the saddle, still talking to the horse in his soothing tones.

He sat there for a brief period as if he was gathering his thoughts, and then gently touched a heel to the horse's side. I noticed he wasn't wearing spurs and wondered if I should have taken mine off.

When he touched the horse's side, the horse made another giant leap into the air. I heard some muffled cuss words as the horse came down and went up again. This time, when he came down, he remained still, although he was quivering.

"He's okay now," said the rancher. "Let's go!"

We started out at a slow trot and I watched the rancher's horse closely. He was a little reluctant to move out and was fighting his head some as the rancher gently tried to control him. "This horse he's ridin' needs some real work done on him. A lot of ground work and a lot of wet saddle blankets. Lots of wet saddle blankets makes for a good horse," I thought.

The horse I had been given to ride was well mannered and responded well to any command.

I'd heard that about wet saddle blankets making a good horse before and thought I might mention it to the rancher just to show off my knowledge of horses. Then I thought better of it. If I showed that I knew a lot, the rancher might become more insistent on my going to work for him.

Soon the rancher had the horse under more control, and we slowed our pace to a walk.

"He just needs more ridin'," said the rancher.

"More ground work wouldn't hurt," I volunteered.

"That'll come," replied the rancher. "This horse will be used an' he can learn while he's bein' used. On the job training is the best!"

We made small talk as we rode to the sheep. As we got close, I could hear the ringing of the bells he'd put on some ewes to make finding the flock easier. And I could smell the sheep. I didn't think the small of sheep was all that unpleasant, but I didn't think I wanted to be around it all the time.

A whistle from the rancher brought his dogs. I was surprised. I was looking for Border Collies, but three big white dogs appeared.

"What kind of dogs are those? I ain't never seen anything like them."

"Great Pyrenees," was the reply. "Best sheepdogs on earth. They guard them sheep better than I can. And they can move in the herd without disturbing the flock. The sheep ain't even scared of 'em. I guess the sheep think they're one of them."

The rancher got off his horse and the horse stepped back a step or two. The dogs were obviously glad to see the rancher and he rewarded them by giving each a strip of bacon left over from breakfast.

"We'll make a trip around the flock and move 'em up toward the mountain a little. They've about used up all the feed here."

The rancher stepped toward his horse and the horse backed away again. I had the feeling that the horse didn't really trust the rider, and that he hadn't been rode that much in the past.

Using the same soothing tones that he used before, the rancher got on his horse. The horse was still on guard, but he didn't jump like he did before.

"I guess I should do that all day to get him used to people, but I got other things to do," said the rancher, as we slowly headed around the sheep. "You head 'round that way an' push the sheep in that direction an' I'll go 'round this way an' head 'em where they're supposed to go. Just take 'em slow. Don't let 'em drift off the ridge. We want 'em towards the top of that ridge over there."

He pointed toward the ridge where he wanted the sheep.

"That'll take us all day to get there," I said.

"What else we got to do today?"

We parted and I got to thinking, "I was offered a job, which I refused, an' now am workin' for the outfit I refused to work for. Have I been hood-winked? Well, he did save my burros, or in his words, jackasses, so I guess I do owe him something. An' he did give me breakfast, which I didn't much want, even though it was pretty good."

I was debating my situation in my mind, slowly moving the sheep up the mountain. I could camp there tonight, and then move on in the morning. I wasn't in a big rush—Sassy hadn't slowed me down that much. As she had gotten a few days older, she did a better job of keeping up, and tying her to Sally had increased her speed considerably.

I kept an eye on the sheep—they didn't try to drift off the ridge and they seemed to know we were headed for fresh feed. I did see the rancher on the other side of the herd, moving alongside the flock. I thought we were getting the job done.

After a couple of hours, the rancher rode over to me. "We'll let 'em go from here," he said. "We'll go back to camp an' call it a day. I've got to come back an' feed the dogs. You can take it easy for the rest of the day. Then we'll go huntin'."

He was giving me orders just like I was on the payroll. And hunting? It wasn't hunting season.

As we rode back to camp, I started a conversation with the rancher. "I suppose I'll head out in the morning. I really have to be back in school on time to maintain my perfect attendance record."

I didn't have a perfect attendance record—I'd sluffed school a lot to stay on the ranch and help with the more fun jobs.

"But we haven't got the sheep moved yet," said the rancher. "We've still got a few miles to go, then we'll have to move camp. We ain't done."

"Wait a minute," I said. "You offered me a job, an' I didn't take it. But you saved my jackasses an' I figured I owed you, so I helped you today. But I'm not lookin' for a job, I've got to get back to school!"

I was interrupted. "You'll learn more out here than you will in school!"

"That might be right," I conceded, "but I do have other obligations."

The rancher smiled. "I guess you're right. But I do need some help moving these sheep. You think it over while we're huntin'."

"What are we huntin'?" I was anxious to change the subject. I was beginning to get an idea of why the rancher's help had quit—he was overbearing.

"Venison."

"It ain't deer season," I said.

"Yes it is."

"No," I said, "it's too early."

"Not for archery an' muzzleloader," said the rancher.

"You got one?"

"Yep. It's loaded an' primed an' ready too go. We'll be eatin' heart, liver an' taters tonight for supper."

This rancher was being extra nice to me, it seemed like. However, I was determined not to go to work for him. And even though he'd offered me a job, he hadn't mentioned anything about how much he'd pay.

We got back to his camp. It was starting to get late in the day and the rancher changed his plans.

"I'll get some dog food, and we'll feed the dogs, then go huntin'."

The rancher handed me the reins to his horse, went into his sheep wagon and returned with a twenty-two rifle and a gunny sack of dry dog food. He put the rifle in an empty scabbard on his saddle and tied the dog food to the saddle strings just below the swells on the front of the saddle. His horse had calmed down considerably with the riding during the day, and he didn't act at all like he did in the morning.

"Let's go," he said, as he got in the saddle, "it's gettin' late."

We started out at a trot, at a faster clip than we had started out at in the morning. I got to thinking that perhaps we were going to move the sheep again and perhaps he was going to try and get more free work out of me.

When we reached the sheep, the rancher whistled and shortly the dogs appeared. He scattered the dry dog food on the ground in three separate piles.

"That's done. Now let's go huntin'."

We started out at a right angle from the direction we had come from.

"The deer won't be close to the sheep," said the rancher. "I think we'll have better luck finding a deer up by them aspens." He pointed in the direction of some trees that looked to be about a mile away.

"Why didn't you bring the dog food out with you this morning? Looks like to me you could have saved yourself a lot of time." I was making idle conversation, trying to figure out if this rancher was still trying to convince me to work for him. The rancher just ignored me.

We reached the aspens, got off our horses and tied them up on the edge of the trees.

"You just follow me," whispered the rancher. "There's some deer in here an' we'll get one. Be quiet."

We entered the aspens quietly. I was watching where I was putting my feet, careful to not put them on a twig and make a noise. Suddenly the rancher's hand came up against my chest. With the rifle he pointed ahead of us.

There was a nice forked-horn buck standing about forty yards away. Slowly he raised the rifle and squeezed the trigger. The buck went down immediately and suddenly the aspens were alive with other deer running away at the sound of the shot.

"There was a bigger buck with that herd of deer, but this one will make better eatin'," said the rancher.

"That don't look like a muzzleloader rifle to me," I said.

"It might not be," said the rancher, "but that's camp meat."

It didn't take long to gut the deer and leave the unwanted parts in the trees. We ended up taking the carcass, heart, and liver back with us. We had no use for the legs, head, or anything else but the carcass.

We made good time getting back to camp. I unsaddled the horses, hobbled them, and turned them loose while the rancher started a fire in the sheep wagon, sliced up the heart and liver, sliced some potatoes and started them all cooking in a big frying pan.

While the rancher was fixing supper, I went out to give Roman and Sally their grain. I wanted them close in the morning, just in case I had to make a fast getaway or sneak away.

It wasn't long before the rancher called, "Supper's ready!"

The smell was inviting and supper tasted mighty good that night. While supper was cooking, the rancher had started boning out the deer carcass. I was surprised at how much he had got done. What was left of the deer carcass had been placed in a meat sack and hung on the shady side of the sheep wagon.

While we were eating, a truck drove up. A Forest Service truck. I immediately knew we were going to be arrested for poaching.

"Come on in, Ranger! You can sit a spell an' eat with us!"

A short, stocky, well-built man dressed in the unmistakable uniform of a forest ranger entered the sheep wagon.

The rancher reached for a plate, filled it up with a couple of scoops of liver, heart, and potatoes from the frying pan and set it down next to his plate. He then moved his own stuff over, allowing the ranger to sit next to him.

"There's a knife an' fork in that drawer," said the rancher, pointing to a drawer in the end of the fold-up table.

The ranger got a knife and fork from the drawer, sat down and started to eat. Up to this point, he hadn't said a word and I decided to keep my mouth shut unless I was spoken to.

Finally the ranger said, "How you doing, boy."

He caught me by surprise.

"I'm good," I said.

The ranger continued, "I heard about you from the sheriff. You making out all right?

"So far, so good." I was somewhat relieved that I didn't have to repeat my story about where I was going and what I was doing.

The ranger did give me some directions on how to find some good places to camp and find water along my route.

"When you leaving?"

"About daylight in the morning," I answered. "This rancher saved my burros from a mountain lion and I felt obliged to help him out today."

"Mountain lion, huh? I thought I heard some rifle shots earlier."

"Yep," said the rancher. "He's been bothering my sheep so I started carrying a rifle."

The rancher and the ranger continued to talk while they ate. I ate and listened. Their talk didn't amount to much—weather, deer numbers, range conditions, and the like. Finally, the two finished eating.

"I've got to get going," said the ranger. "Let me know if you get that cat. Thanks for supper. Let me know if you see any suspicious activity, like poaching. You know, you do raise the best mutton around."

The ranger had a half-way smile on his face as he made the last comment.

"Come anytime, Fred. You're always welcome," said the rancher.

It occurred to me that these two guys knew each other, and probably pretty good.

"I'm goin' to hit the sack," I said. "I'll be goin' in the morning, an' I need to get an early start."

"You can go anytime you want," said the rancher. "Coffee, it'll be ready before the sun comes up. You're welcome to it."

I checked on Roman and Sally and Sassy again and turned in for the night. As I lay in my bedroll, I did a lot of thinking. I suppose it would have been proper to stick around and help the rancher, but once again I had lost track of time and wasn't even sure of what day it was and how much time I had to get home. If I could time it right, I'd have a day or two to buy school clothes and relax some.

I woke up early the next morning and caught up Roman

and Sally. I could hear some stirring in the sheep wagon and saw smoke coming from the smokestack.

I got Roman and Sally saddled and loaded. While I was packing Sally, the rancher stuck his head out the door and hollered, "Coffee's ready!"

I had a shock. The rancher was bald! He had hair around his head where his hat set, but none on top. His white head made a striking contrast to his tanned face and he looked somewhat comical sticking his head out the door in the semi darkness of early morning. It occurred to me that this morning was the first time I had seen him with his hat off.

The coffee was good that morning and the company even better than the day before. The rancher had apparently given up on his idea of me going to work for him.

I thanked him for the coffee and supper the night before and added, "You know, it was kinda fun to feed that ranger some of his own meat and him not even knowin' it! I thought that was real interestin'."

"Oh, he knew it! You can't put much over on my brother."

Brother! That's why nothing was said about the venison! And, I was beginning to think everyone in this county was related.

I headed out with mixed feelings. But I did have my own schedule, regardless of how flexible it might be.

A Change of Pace

The next few days were pretty much alike—ride in the morning, take a little break around midday if I was in an area where there was feed and water, then ride in the afternoon, make camp and hit the sack. I was totally accustomed to the routine. My supplies were holding up pretty good, although I would need to replenish them shortly.

I did notice Roman had a loose shoe and as I inspected his other feet, I determined that he would need reshoeing pretty soon. I got a couple of rocks and tried to tighten up his loose shoe, but without much success. Shoeing equipment! Something else I needed, but had completely overlooked.

I resolved to myself that next time I did something like this, I'd be better prepared! "That sheep rancher had said I'd learn more out here than in school an' I guess he was right! I'm learning that I should do more planning," I said to myself, grinning.

I was seeing more and more irrigated pastures from a distance, but I was staying pretty close to or on the Forest Service property. The directions the forest ranger had given me were good and I didn't have a problem finding water for my horse and burros.

Sassy was growing and starting to eat some grass, she'd been nibbling at it for some time. I'd started giving her a little grain when I grained Roman and Sally in the morning and at night. She was keeping up better and was becoming somewhat of a nuisance when I was packing Sally in the morning.

Even though I thought it kind funny at times, most of the time she was in the way.

I was heading out of the forest one morning, along a forest service road, when I came across a herd of cows. There were about fifty cows and calves and they were being herded by about twenty people. These cows were being driven by a bunch of the best-dressed cowboys and cowgirls I'd ever seen. And some of the people were right up in the middle of the cows!

"Howdy stranger!" The greeting came from a well-dressed cowboy, riding a big, well built paint horse. "Where you headed?"

"I'm headed north," I said, admiring the horse. The horse actually looked like he'd been manicured as slick as the cowboy was.

"How far?"

"'Till I get home," I replied.

"Seems like I heard about you, going home horseback with a couple of burros."

"That'd be me," I said. I was slightly getting used to being a celebrity, and not surprised that I was achieving a little reputation.

"Just turn your burros loose and we'll drive them with the cows. We've only got another mile or so and we're going to stop and have a little lunch. You might just as well join us."

Once again I was being ordered and I didn't know if I liked

it or not. But, knowing I was starting to get short on supplies, I thought it might be a good idea to join the cattle drive and get a free meal.

"I'm Bud Wilson," said the guy on the big paint horse. "I own this outfit."

I told him my name, then asked, "What kind of outfit is this? You got almost as many hands as you got cows an' they're the best-dressed hands I ever seen, except at a rodeo. An' they're all ridin' good horses."

It occurred to me, when I heard this guy's name that I hadn't found out the names of any of the people I had met on the trail. I thought that perhaps I was lacking in social skills. Then I thought, "I really don't need many social skills out here. I only talk to myself and Roman and Sally. I had started to talk to Sassy, but only because she was in the way so much and I was becoming annoyed with her. My comments to her generally weren't of the quality that would be needed in social situations anyway."

"We got a few more cows than what you see here," said Mister Wilson. "We're a working cow ranch and a dude ranch."

"A dude ranch?" The question slipped out without me thinking about it. I'd heard about dude ranches but had never seen one or been on one.

"Yep," said Mister Wilson. "With the exception of Patrick up there in front, these so-called hands are all dudes."

"Mister Wilson," I asked, "is that why some of 'em are in the middle of the herd?"

"It's Bud, son. We're not so formal out here. And that's exactly right. These people are from cities back East and they come out here to play cowboy for a week or so. Sometimes they get a pretty good education, not only about cowboys, cows and horses, but about life."

"They pay you for bein' a cowboy?"

"They don't pay me for being a cowboy," said Bud, "they pay me so that they can have the opportunity to actually be a cowboy and do a cowboy's work for a week or so."

"Sounds like a good deal," I said. "And they pay you to do your work for you."

"That's the way it's supposed to work, but sometimes they create extra work. Turn your jackasses loose and you can help push these cows to a new pasture. Some of these dudes are neglecting their duties and coming back here to see what you're doing."

I had noticed we were starting to gather a crowd and the cattle were starting to scatter. I turned Sally and Sassy loose, and started to push cows.

These dudes were very friendly, each one of them greeting me with "Howdy!" They sounded very phony and I thought they were trying to perfect their western persona. Some of them would go a little further and add their name to their "Howdy!" The addition of their names didn't mean much to me. I didn't think I could remember them all anyway.

I started trying to make a semblance of a cow herd out of the mess I had encountered. Bud didn't seem to mind the confusion, but he kept the cattle headed in the right direction. The dudes added more work than help for the most part, but a few of them did have a little cow savvy, and were quite helpful.

Pushing the herd, once we finally got them moving right, I noticed some of the dudes. One lady seemed to be following one cow, not paying any attention to the other cattle. She seemed determined to follow that one cow and was right in the middle of the herd.

With her being in the middle of the herd, she was scattering cattle a little to both sides. Patrick was having a tough time up front keeping the cattle going in the direction he wanted them to go. The cattle wanted to go west and Patrick wanted them to go east. Bud had slipped around on the west side of the herd to give Patrick a hand.

Seeing what was happening, I hollered at the woman, "Get out of the middle of them cows, Dude! You're supposed to be takin' them cows where you want 'em to go, not lettin' 'em take you where they want to go! Get out of there!"

The woman looked at me with a shocked look on her face. I saw Bud and Patrick laughing. I didn't know what I had done, but I suspected a feller wasn't supposed to yell at the dudes. The woman did move to the side of the herd, giving me a dirty look all the way, but she went to the east side causing Bud and Patrick a little more work as the cattle headed west.

Presently the herd was settled and I saw Bud work his way around to the woman I'd yelled at. I suppose he was smoothing over what I had done, from the way he was moving his hands as he talked. I thought I might be in trouble for my actions.

"Well," I thought, "it didn't take much to help out here an' it won't take much to leave. All I had to do was gather up Sally and Sassy and go."

I'd forgot about Sally and Sassy, but there was no need for concern, they were following the cattle and in turn were being followed by a number of youngsters that had apparently lost interest in following the cattle.

Shortly, Bud worked his way around to me. He edged up beside me and said, "We really don't yell at the guests."

I knew I was in trouble.

"But," he continued, "I suppose I should thank you. That's Misses Abercrombie you yelled at. She's been coming out here for years and has always been in the way. Today is the first day we actually haven't had to work around her. We tolerate her because she pays good money to come out here and help us."

There was an ironic grin on Bud's face as he made his last comment, leading me to believe she hadn't been that much help over the years.

"Also," continued Bud, "we don't call the dudes, Dudes. They're actually guests!"

"Why not call a spade a spade?"

"That's just kinda the way we do things," said Bud. "And the money involved makes it no trouble at all. We're almost to where we want to be for lunch, only a mile or so to go. We'll turn the cattle through the gate and get something to eat."

I asked, "Aren't you going to mother up the cattle?"

"No need to. With the gate closed, the lost calves can't go back. They'll find their moms right here at the gate."

I'd always been taught to mother up the cows and their calves before leaving a herd of cattle. The cows and calves will generally go back to the last place where the calf had sucked to find each other when they get separated. But with the gate closed, there didn't appear to be a need to do this.

"What about water?"

"There's water down over that hill. These cows have been here before, they know where it is," answered Bud.

The cattle were pretty well lined out, so I fell in behind them, where I could keep an eye on my burros. We were moving the cattle a little fast and some of the smaller calves were starting to lag behind. I took down my lariat rope and began to heel some of the calves. I didn't dally up; I just set the trap for their hind feet, and let them walk through it. I hadn't done any roping since I had left my job, and this little exercise was just for practice. My shoulder and wrist felt pretty good and I thought I'd give them a good test. They appeared to be all right.

I did notice that none of the calves were branded.

I noticed Bud watching me, but he didn't say anything as I wasn't causing any harm. A few of the dudes, that is guests, were also watching me and Bud took down his own rope, made a big loop, tied a knot around the honda so that if one of the dudes caught something, the loop wouldn't tighten up, and gave the rope to one of the dudes. Patrick also did the same thing, and we had a couple of the dudes trying to rope the heels of the cattle.

Soon we reached the lunch area. A cook was present and he'd brought his supplies out by truck, had a fire going, and lunch was almost ready.

The cattle were turned loose through the gate. I caught up Sally and hobbled her, then un-hobbled her and led her farther away from the site and hobbled her again.

Bud and Patrick were tying the dude's horses to the fence-posts. I'd had to move Sally farther away from the tied horses. I didn't want her or Roman getting mixed up with the tied horses, which might cause a wreck.

I hobbled Roman, and we were a good distance away from the tied horses. Looking at the distance I had to walk to the eating area, I decided to take off my chaps to walk over. These bat-wing chaps were difficult to walk in and I did have some brush to walk through.

As I approached the eating area, I immediately became aware of the dirty clothes I was wearing when contrasted to the new clothes of the dudes. I became somewhat embarrassed.

Bud noticed this, but chose to ignore my situation. "Grab a plate and something to eat," he said.

I did as told, and was surprised at the food that was offered. Potato salad, all kinds of sliced cold cuts—beef, turkey, ham—home-made sourdough bread, and two kinds of pie—apple and cherry. There was also ice-cold lemonade in a big five gallon thermos.

I waited until the guests had filled their plates and then followed Patrick through the line. There was plenty and I wasn't bashful about loading up my plate. I followed Patrick to the outer edge of the circle that the dudes had formed.

Bud had a full plate and walked around the dude's circle, checking on each person and getting a mouthful of food between comments. After making some small talk with each guest, he came over to where Patrick and I were seated, and joined us.

"You look to be fairly handy with that rope," he said.

Immediately, I thought I was in trouble.

"I haven't used it for the last month or so," I said. "I thought a little practice wouldn't hurt nothin' an' I didn't dally up." I was feeling guilty.

"That didn't hurt nothing," said Bud. "In fact, some of the guests wanted to try it. Patrick and I had to set things up right for them and they had some fun.

"Maybe you noticed that none of those calves are branded. We're fixing to have a branding tomorrow, why don't you stick around for a few days and give us a hand? We'll show these guests how it's really done. Besides that, your horse could use some shoeing and I've got a horseshoer coming to reset some of my horses. I'd pay you some cash and cover your horseshoeing bill and give you room and board. You could also help entertain these guests at night, and take advantage of our swimming pool, after you've had a shower. In fact, we've got a square dance scheduled for tonight and that will be a lot of fun."

I immediately became aware of just how dirty I actually was and became selfconscious about it.

"How many days do you think it will take me to get cleaned up? I mean, how many days do you want me to help you out?"

"It should only be three or four," answered Bud. "Four at the most. You might even want to get some new clothes and some supplies from our gift shop. I'd make you a good deal on whatever you wanted."

"Are you sure you want me around after I yelled at that dude … er, ah, guest this morning?"

"That's all right," said Bud. "I talked to her. She's really a nice lady and quite anxious to meet you personally!"

"I can't believe that," I said. "The look she gave me after I yelled at her really wasn't very nice."

"Don't let that bother you. Some of these wealthy people have some strange ways and they're used to yelling at people rather than being yelled at. This is their vacation time and they just want to have some fun. There's no reason why we can't have fun right along with them."

This offer was starting to sound a little too good to be true. But it was more inviting than what the sheep rancher had offered me.

"I could help you out for three or four days, at the most, but I do have to get back in time for school and early enough to do a little shopping for school."

I did feel a little guilty about taking this job when I had turned the sheep rancher's job offer down, but this sure looked to be lots more fun.

"I've heard all about that," said Bud. "You've got time to spend four days here and still make it in time for school."

I was surprised that news about me was traveling around the country faster than I was, and I wondered what was causing all the concern. I figured I was all right.

"When we get to the ranch, I'll show you where you can bunk, and where you can turn your horse and burros loose. They'll have their own little pasture and they'll be close to the ranch."

The deal being done and everyone about done eating, we started to get the guests on their horses. I gathered up Roman and Sally and tied Sassy to Sally. I could lead them to the ranch, it would be easier than trying to drive them, and especially with all the help we had.

The ride back to the ranch was leisurely, with various riders pairing and grouping themselves together. I was content to trail along behind them, but Sassy was drawing a lot of attention and I was soon surrounded by dudes, that is, guests. They were mostly the younger kids, some of them being about my own age, I guessed. There were a few parents joining us, probably to watch out for their youngsters.

Shortly, we reached the ranch. I was somewhat taken back by its appearance. A big lodge, where I suspected the meals were served, surrounded by neat little cabins and they were all surrounded by freshly manicured lawn. The barn and corrals were off to the side. The place looked like a resort to me and I had only seen pictures of them in magazines.

"Looks like a resort to me," I said to Roman.

"That's what it is, son."

I hadn't seen Bud ride up beside me and his comment startled me.

"It is kinda pretty," he said, as we stopped a moment and surveyed the scene. I could tell he was proud of it.

I had to agree with him. "I don't think I've seen anything like it," I said, as we continued on.

"You follow me and I'll show you where you can put your

things and your horse and burros. You know, your burros have raised quite a stir among the younger riders."

Obediently, I followed.

We passed the bunkhouse, and Bud said, "You can put your stuff in there when you unpack your burro. There's a couple of bunks in there that aren't being used, just pick whichever one you want. You can unsaddle your critters by the barn over there and turn them loose in the north pasture, next to the jingle horse's pasture. There's plenty of feed and water there, they'll be okay in there for a couple of days.

"You can put your saddle on one of the racks that doesn't have a name on it."

"Names on saddle racks?" I was curious. At home we put our saddles on racks and just got our own saddles when we needed them.

"Yep. Every horse on this outfit has a name and his own saddle rack," said Bud. "Each horse will get the same saddle every day. Cuts down on saddle sores when the saddle is fitted correctly."

That made sense to me and I could begin to see that Bud really knew what he was doing in this business.

"When you get everything put away, you can grab a shower and get ready for supper. We'll eat promptly at six."

It was becoming readily apparent that I was pretty dirty and in need of some clean clothes. Some of Bud's comments were a thinly disguised suggestion that I could be a little cleaner.

"I've got some clean clothes in my pack, but I don't have a towel," I said. "Any chance I could borrow one?"

"Sure," said Bud. "Anything else you might need, just ask."

"A bar of soap might help," I added.

Bud laughed. "Certainly! It sure would! It doesn't do any

good to shower without soap! I'll have someone bring them down."

Bud left, laughing, and I didn't know if he was laughing at me or my request.

I took Sally back to the bunkhouse and unloaded the panniers there. Then I took her and Roman to the barn and unsaddled them and turned them into the pasture as instructed. Then I headed back to the bunkhouse to set up my own housekeeping.

I unpacked both panniers in the bunkhouse. I found my clean pants and a clean, but wrinkled shirt and set them on an unused bunk. I found clean underwear and socks and set them with the pants and shirt. The other items, groceries and the like, I left in the panniers.

Then, I made an exploratory trip around the bunkhouse. There was plenty of room and it looked like there were a few extra bunks that weren't being used. I found the bathroom and the shower, and turned on the hot water. There appeared to be plenty.

There was a knock at the door and I went to answer it. Before I could get to the door, it opened and a young girl stuck her head inside and asked, "Anybody here?"

"Over here," I said.

"I'm Sally, and I was told to bring this to you."

She handed me a big, fluffy towel and a new bar of soap.

"That's strange," I said. "I have a ..."

I paused.

"What's strange?"

"I was goin' to say, I have a jackass named Sally. This might get to be confusing."

"And I'll bet she's a beautiful jackass," said Sally.

"Most assuredly," I said, "most assuredly."

I could tell that this Sally thought she was cute and I would have to agree with her. I figured her to be about my own age, give or take a year or two.

"I still have work to do," Sally said, as she turned to leave. "Don't forget to wash behind your ears!"

I took a little offense at her remark, but she left so fast I didn't have time to say anything. I was at that awkward age, thinking myself already a man, yet still being perceived as a boy.

I took the towel and soap and headed back to the bathroom. I did need a shower, so I stripped down. I got the water at the hottest temperature I could stand and stepped in. That was a little too hot, so I added some cold.

I really enjoyed that shower. I was fascinated watching the dust and dirt wash down the drain and I hadn't even used the soap yet. Yes, I was dirty and I began to wonder if all that dirt going down the drain would plug up the drain pipes. I thought if I used the soap, it might help dilute the dirt and make draining the shower easier. So the soap got used and the dirt really flowed off.

I washed my hair and was surprised at how dirty the water got when I rinsed. I didn't think my head got that dirty, I wore a hat all the time!

Satisfied that I was as clean as I was going to get, and convinced that any more scrubbing was bound to take off my hide, I just stood there and let the water run over me.

When I'd had enough and not wanting to be late for supper, I turned off the water, dried off and started to get dressed. I was just tucking in my shirt when there was another knock on the door.

Before I could open it, the door opened and Sally asked, "You coming to supper?"

"I'm ready now," I said.

"Good," said Sally. "I'll take you to the dining room."

The dining room was set up in a buffet style. It was serve yourself. I saw the sign, "TAKE ALL YOU WANT, BUT EAT ALL YOU TAKE." I made sure I didn't take more than I could eat.

Sally instructed me. "Get a tray here, a plate here, silverware here, and just pick out what you want." She was even kind enough to show me how to fill my plate as she filled hers.

Occasionally, she would ask, "Do you want some of this?"

When I said no, she simply put it on her plate.

I followed Sally down the line and when we got to the end, she said, "Follow me. You can sit with us."

I sat down at Sally's table, off in the corner, with some other people about our own ages. I thought they were hired help, but they turned out to be the sons and daughters of the guests. They were guests themselves.

There was a lot of small talk among the teenagers, and I didn't have the opportunity to say much. There were a few questions about Sassy, but the abrupt manner in which I answered them discouraged any more questions.

I did manage to ask Sally, "What's your job here?"

Before she could answer, one of the teenage boys that I had figured for a loudmouth shouted out, "She's a maid, an unofficial greeter, and a gofer!"

All the teenagers laughed. Sally didn't seem upset.

"That's right," said Sally. "I do about everything around here that needs to be done. Go for this, go for that, I do it all."

"She's one of our most valuable employees," said Bud.

I hadn't seen him come up and was unaware he was present until he spoke. He had a knack for getting up close to someone without them knowing it. But his being present gave me the opportunity to ask a question or two myself.

"How'd you come to be in this business?" I asked. I was curious how such a nice resort could be out in the middle of nowhere like this one.

"I was born and raised on this ranch," said Bud. "The old cabin my grandfather built is no longer standing; this lodge is built where it stood. There are some old artifacts from that era decorating this dining room."

I looked around the room and saw some old saddles, bridles, and pictures placed in various spots.

Bud continued, "My grandfather raised cattle here for years, and he always had a little band of sheep around. He said the sheep were more profitable than the cattle because you got two crops from them—lambs and wool."

It became obvious that Bud liked talking about his ranch.

"My dad was killed in the war, and my two brothers and myself tried to make a go of raising cattle. We had some tough years and finally, one of my brothers took the sheep and a couple of sections of land to the south. I didn't have any money to buy him out, so he settled for the land. The other brother got a job with the government, and I'm still buying him out.

"When the price of cattle got so low it looked like I would have to sell out, I went to the bank with this plan to make a dude ranch out of this place to get two crops off the land—calves and dudes. The bank went for the idea so we built this facility. We've been adding on slowly, one cabin at a time, and now we're almost where we want to be.

"We've added the dudes so we can continue to run the cows. We've got about three hundred head of cows, seventy-five or so horses, a big staff, most of it summertime help. We can take guests for about eight months out of the year and can house about forty-five guests at a time. The dudes have really enabled us to stay in the cow business."

"Are you related to that sheepherder rancher a few days ride from here?"

"Yes," was Bud's reply. "And his brother, the forest ranger, is also my other brother."

Now I was sure of it, everyone in this county was related!

"What relation are you to the county sheriff? And the highway patrolman?"

"None that I know of," answered Bud. "But I do know them quite well. Why do you ask?"

"Just curious," I said. "For a while I thought everyone in this part of the country was related."

"There's going to be a square dance a little later, over in the recreation hall. I expect we'll see you there," said Bud.

"I don't really know how to square ..."

"I'll show you," interrupted Sally. "That's part of my job here."

If Sally was going to teach me how to square dance, she was certainly going to earn her wages.

"I'd best be goin' out to get some fresh air," I said. I was really looking to get away from the other teenagers. They had become quite loud and I'd thought they hadn't shown Bud the proper respect while he was telling me the history of the ranch.

"I'll take you around and introduce you to everyone," said Sally.

"But ..."

Once again I was interrupted.

"You'll need to know everyone so you'll know who you're dancing with tonight."

Sally grabbed my hand and started to lead me around to the guests. I was surprised at how she could remember everyone's name. I'd forgotten most of the names right after I'd been told them. I also met the other hired help.

There were two other wranglers besides Patrick, a cook and a cook's helper, four maids, a handyman that doubled as a chauffeur and a fishing guide.

I also met Misses Abercrombie. I was somewhat embarrassed meeting her formally. This was the lady I had yelled at earlier in the day and called a dude.

"You're quite outspoken, aren't you young man?" Misses Abercrombie spoke with a very pronounced New England accent. She appeared to be very proper and I felt out of place.

"Yes," I said, forgetting to add the proper title. And I would have added the proper title if I knew what it was. "I don't believe in hiding anything."

I knew I was lying when I said it. I was wishing right then I could go somewhere and hide myself.

"Well don't you ever change, young man! We need more people that aren't afraid to speak their mind. And you know," she said, with a wink and a grin, "that cow that I followed never did escape!"

I had to laugh. "No she didn't," I said.

I had met everyone and knew I couldn't remember their names, everyone except Misses Abercrombie. I was sure I'd never forget her.

"I need to go outside, get some fresh air an' sit down," I said.

"I'll go with you," said Sally. "It is a little stuffy in here."

"You don't have to," I said. "You probably have to entertain the dudes, er ... guests."

"No. They'll be all right."

Sally was sticking pretty close to me and I was having some misgivings. Was this part of her job or did she have other intentions? I'd never had a girl friend before, not since I was in the first grade anyways, and I wasn't sure just what I should do. While she was really a cute girl, I just didn't want that much to do with her. But, I got to thinking, I did like being around her.

We sat outside the recreation hall until the call was made that the dance was starting. I was surprised. There was a guitar player, a fiddle player, and a guy with an accordion. Bud had gone to the trouble to bring in a band! Apparently money was no object for the satisfaction of his guests.

The handyman, Richard, was the square dance caller. I had made another miscalculation. The band members were actually guests. The music for the square dance was actually played on a phonograph and the musician guests were just entertaining everyone.

The call was made for the dance to begin. "Grab your partners, its time to start," hollered Richard.

Sally promptly grabbed my hand and dragged me out to the middle of the dance floor. I could feel my face getting redder and redder and I could see some of the other guests concealing their laughter with muffled smiles and giggles. I was becoming quite embarrassed. I didn't know what to do.

The music started, Richard began calling, and I just stood there until Sally grabbed me and kinda flung me around.

"Go left, young man, go left." It was Bud, giving me instructions as he went past me.

"No, your other left," said Patrick, as he went past me.

"Don't you know your left from your right?" It was one of the other wranglers.

"I know my left from my right; I just don't know promenade, or do-see-do or allemande! I gotta get outa here!"

I started to leave, but was occasionally swung around by a square dancer. I finally made it to the side of the dance floor and turned around to watch.

What I saw was what looked like controlled mass confusion. But everyone seemed to know exactly what they were doing and Richard kept calling out instructions. After watching for a while, I felt lucky that I hadn't bumped into somebody and knocked them down, or got knocked down myself.

I slipped outside to catch my breath and Sally followed me.

"You really don't know how to dance, do you?" Sally's tone was almost sympathetic.

"That's what I tried to tell you," I said.

"We can teach you," she said.

"To be perfectly honest with you, I don't think I want to learn. I'm content to just sit an' watch."

"A real wallflower!"

"What's that mean?" I thought I was being insulted.

"Never mind," said Sally, kind of disgustedly.

"I think I'll go to the bunkhouse an' turn in. I'm kinda tired an' I'm used to gettin' up early."

"No, you can't. Bud wants you here."

"So," I thought, "Sally doesn't really have an interest in me. She's just stickin' close to me followin' Bud's orders."

I was relieved at my deduction, but also disappointed. "Why didn't Sally have an interest in me?" I was a very confused young kid.

A couple of more dances and Bud took the microphone from Richard.

"I want to introduce you people to our new hand that I hired to help us out for a couple of days. He came in here horseback and if he isn't careful he'll ride out of here on his ass. He insulted Misses Abercrombie and that's only one of the reasons I hired him. And here he is, Mister ..."

The laughter and hoots of the crowd drowned out my name.

"Come up here son and say a few words."

At Bud's insistence, I walked to the center of the room. Bud gave me the microphone and left.

"I really don't know what to say. For the last month or so all I've had to talk to has been my horse and my burros. And they're not really very good conversationalists."

The crowd laughed at this comment.

"If I'd have known I was going to have to make a speech, I could have practiced on them. But they wouldn't have said anything."

The crowd laughed again, and I began to wonder how much they'd had to drink.

"I've proved to you that I can't dance an' now I've got a chance to prove to you that I'm not a public speaker."

The crowd laughed again and I made up my mind that this crowd had definitely had too much to drink.

After an awkward moment of silence, Bud said, "Tell us how you come to be here, son."

I repeated my story as I had told it many times, and when I got done someone asked, "Did you get lost?"

"No," I said, "I never did get lost. But there were a lot of times when I didn't know just where I was."

The crowd laughed again. They might not have laughed if they had known how truthful my last statement really was.

Bud made his way through the crowd and took the microphone. He asked for a round of applause for his honored guest and I left the spotlight.

When the dancing resumed, I found Bud, apologized for my performance, and told him I was ready to hit the sack.

"There's no need for you to apologize," said Bud. "Those people enjoyed everything you said and I thank you for cooperating."

I turned to leave and Bud said, "The boys will bring in the horses in the morning. You can sleep in."

I slept good that night, only a little concerned that Sally didn't have any intentions toward me.

I woke up early the next morning, but the other hands were already leaving the bunkhouse to gather the horses.

"The coffee's probably ready," said Patrick, as he walked out the door.

I got up, got dressed and went to the kitchen, hoping to get a cup of coffee. The cook was jovial and allowed me to get a big cup.

"Can I take this down to the corral?"

"Yes," said the cook, "but make sure you bring the cup back."

"You bet," I said, as I left for the corral. I could hear a couple of the fellers hollering at the horses and saw some dust they were raising. Soon I could hear the horses' hooves pounding on the ground.

It was kinda fun to watch the horses being brought in on a run. I wondered why the guests weren't up and watching this. I checked the cabins and there were some guests in various degrees of nightwear standing on the porches watching. Some of them were already dressed and when the horses were corralled, they started for the kitchen looking for their coffee.

The wranglers closed the corral gate and started toward the barn.

"Good morning, World Famous!"

It was Sally. She had gone out with the wranglers and helped bring in the horses. I could see why Bud called her the most valuable employee on the place; it appeared she could do anything that needed doing. The reaction of the loud-mouthed teenager the night before may have had its beginnings in jealousy. This gal apparently could do everything and probably better than him.

I was taken back by her greeting. I had no idea I was famous, much less world famous.

"Good morning," I said. "What's with the World Famous?"

I followed her in the barn.

"You made quite a hit with your speech last night," she said.

"No. Those folks just had too much to drink. They'd have laughed if I'd have told them I was the President of the United States or a visitor from Mars."

"That's probably true," said Sally, as she smiled and unsaddled her horse.

"You help bring in the horses every morning?"

"As often as I can," she replied. "It's the best time of the day and it's fun to bring them in at a run."

"I'll see if I can help saddle," I said.

"I've got other work to do," said Sally as she left. "See you at breakfast."

I asked Patrick, "What can I do to help?"

"We know the horses and where their saddles are. Why don't you brush? The brushes and curry combs are over there," he said, pointing to a box nailed to the wall. "Make sure you brush 'em good, they need to look pretty for the dudes."

"Don't you mean guests?"

"Yeah," answered Patrick, "guests." He was grinning as he made that comment.

94

Shortly after we started saddling, Bud came down to the barn. "We'll need about everything saddled this morning. We're going to brand those calves we gathered and moved yesterday and everybody wants to come and help. Put him," he said, pointing at me, "on Drygulch."

Drygulch! I didn't know if I liked the sound of that or not. They caught up the horse and I saddled him.

"Let's go get something to eat," someone said.

We started toward the kitchen. "Tell me about this horse, Drygulch."

I was trying to find out if I was going to get dry-gulched or not.

"He's not a bad horse," said Patrick. "I've used him quite a bit myself. He don't get used much because he's not as pretty as the other horses. But he'll do the job, and have plenty left over at the end of the day. He's just a little barn sour."

There was some time to kill after breakfast, as not all the guests got up early. When everyone that was going showed up, we got them mounted and started out. Getting the dudes mounted was a chore. Each horse had to be held by a wrangler while the dude got on. This, I was told, was for safety purposes. Bud didn't want any of the horses to move while the dudes were getting on. That's kind of an awkward time, and some of the horses did take a step or two when the dudes pulled themselves into the saddle, just to keep their own balance.

When everyone was mounted, I got on Drygulch and was ready to go. Drygulch was barn sour, but a couple of good hard smacks on his rump with the end of my reins, and he lined right out.

As we left the corral, with Patrick leading the bunch, Bud rode up beside me. "We really don't whip on these horses in front of the guests," he said. "It makes for poor public relations."

"I didn't know," I said. In the short time I had been here, apparently I had broken every rule I didn't know about. "Do I apologize to the guests or the horse?"

Bud laughed. "Neither one. What you did was right and it didn't really hurt the horse, and look at how nice he's lined out. However, all of our actions might be interpreted differently by the guests. We just need to always be aware."

"I'll try to remember," I said. In my mind, I was wondering just how much I could be aware.

We reached the pasture where we turned the cattle loose the day before. "There's a big corral at the end of this pasture," said Bud. "We'll put the cattle in there and start our branding. You," pointing at me, "can be our roper. Don't forget to dally up!"

Bud's comment was an obvious reference to my roping the day before, when I was heeling some calves and not dallying up. He was smiling when he said it, and I thought perhaps I was in his good graces.

The cattle were gathered and put in the corral. A fire was built, the branding irons were put in the fire and we were ready to start, as soon as the irons got hot. The horses were tied outside the corral. While we were waiting for the irons to get hot, Bud told the group, "This young man will be our roper. Everyone that wants to will have a chance to rope, but there will only be two ropers in the corral at a time. We'll need a couple of people to help out on the ground, good stout people."

The loud-mouthed kid volunteered to help on the ground.

Bud asked him, "Don't you want a chance to rope?"

"Nope," he replied.

I wondered why he didn't want to rope, then I saw Sally riding up to help. I figured this loud-mouth had some designs on

Sally, and declined to rope so he wouldn't embarrass himself in front of her.

One of the adults took a try at roping. When the irons got hot, we were ready. The dudes that weren't helping on the ground seated themselves on the fence to watch. I built a loop with my lariat rope and went out to catch a calf.

My first loop missed and I heard the hoo-rah and laughter from the spectators.

"I can do that," said the adult roper. And he did just that, his first loop missed also, much to the delight of the crowd.

"You're setting a bad example," he told me.

"I'll try to do better," I said.

I caught both hind legs on my next loop and dragged the calf up to the fire. I was surprised by the applause that followed my catching the calf. The tourists were getting involved. I looked over at Bud and the smile on his face indicated he was pleased.

Patrick showed the loud-mouthed kid how to roll the calf over to the proper side for branding, and how to hold the calf with his right knee on the calf's neck and holding the calf's left front leg, back towards him. It was a little complicated for the loud-mouth, but he soon got the idea.

One of the other wranglers did the branding and Bud did the earmarking and castrating. Patrick did the vaccinating. When the calf was done, I gave my rope some slack, the calf jumped up, kicked the rope off his heels, and ran back to the herd. I coiled my rope, built a loop, and went out to catch another calf.

The wrangler doing the branding said as I headed out, "We need to hurry up. At this rate, the fire will melt the irons before we're done!" I knew he was only kidding.

"It'll go faster when everyone learns his job," I said, referring to the loud-mouthed teenager.

I caught another calf and dragged him up to the fire. The loud-mouth was still having difficulty with the correct positioning to hold the calf down and I found it kinda comical to watch him. He was struggling and even Sally was smiling at his efforts.

The other roper hadn't caught anything and he volunteered to quit and let someone else try. One of the other guests said, "I'll give it a try, but I don't know if I can catch anything."

We continued branding throughout the morning. None of the guests caught anything, but they were having fun. A couple of them even roped their own horses when they'd get their loops out of control. The loud-mouth working on the ground was working up a sweat, but he wouldn't give up.

We had a little more than half the calves branded when one of the guests caught a calf, around its neck, but he couldn't get his dallies and the calf got away dragging the rope. He still got a big round of applause from the spectators, even though he didn't have a calf.

He looked at me with a proud but sheepish look on his face and said, "I lost my rope."

"I'll get him," I said, "after they get done with this calf."

"No, I'll get him." It was Sally. She'd got her horse and had entered the corral.

I hadn't seen Sally enter the corral—I'd been busy watching the ground crew and keeping the right amount of tension on the rope to help keep the calf down.

But when she built a loop and started after the calf that had got away, I couldn't help but watch. The ground crew turned my calf loose and someone said, "Go catch another one."

I heard him, but I was busy watching Sally. She certainly

knew what she was doing and she had done this before. I wondered, "Is there anything she couldn't do?"

Sally caught her calf on the first loop, turned her horse as she took her dallies and dragged her calf to the fire. She looked very professional.

"Very nice," I said as I passed her, heading out to catch another calf. "Very nice!"

She nodded her head in acknowledgement and continued to drag her calf to the fire.

I caught another calf, but I only had one hind leg. I dragged him to the fire and as I passed Sally heading back to the herd, she said, "Both hind feet, both hind feet!"

"I know. I guess I'm only half as good as you."

Actually, I had pretty much caught both hind feet all morning and when I only had one foot, I tried to let the calf go. I'd done fairly well that morning. I'd missed a few loops, I'd let some go, but by and large I'd had a pretty good day roping.

We were getting close to being done. There were only a few unbranded calves left and they were getting a little wild from having the dudes throw ropes at them.

Bud knew what was happening and he said, "If you have to catch the ones that are left by the head, do it and we'll get done here."

Sally headed out and caught another calf, by the head. The calf was still on his feet as she pulled him to the fire, fighting every inch of the way.

"You're also a header," I said, as she passed me.

"Watch this," she said as she pulled the fighting calf to the loud-mouthed kid.

I watched.

The loud-mouth hadn't had any experience with fighting

calves that were still on their feet and he didn't quite know how to handle the situation. It wasn't long before he had the calf on the ground, but he was under the calf.

"Do you want to brand him that way?" It was Patrick, coming over to help out.

"I'd rather be on top," said the teenager.

The spectacle had brought a lot of laughs from the crowd, and Sally had a big grin on her face.

Patrick got the situation straightened out. When he had the calf on the ground, holding it down by keeping a knee on the calf's neck and his right leg folded up, he took the rope off the neck, put the loop around the calf's hind legs and Sally took the slack out of her rope and held the calf.

"I got him, you take a break," Patrick told the teenager. "You could use a rest."

It was apparent that nobody really cared for the loud-mouthed teenager, but not readily apparent. It was very subtle.

I made another trip through the herd, but couldn't find any unbranded calves.

Bud was counting the ears. "Fifty-two calves we branded today. He marked the number down in a well-worn notebook from his shirt pocket. "There's a cow in this bunch with a little touch of foot rot. Catch her and we'll doctor her while she's here. I've got some penicillin and other medicine in my saddle bags."

"I'll take the head," said Sally. "I know the cow, I saw her earlier."

"Then I'll take the heels," I said.

Sally made a perfect catch on the head and put the cow in perfect position for me to rope the heels. I laid a big trap, and made a perfect catch and we stretched out the cow.

I felt pretty proud as I listened to the applause from the other guests. I didn't know if I was proud of myself or proud of Sally and me, making such a good team.

Bud walked out, gave the cow a shot of penicillin, and sprayed some iodine on the affected foot.

"She's done," Bud said, as he moved to her head to take off Sally's rope.

Sally moved her horse forward a step or two so Bud could take off the rope. I kept the rope tight on the cow's heels to keep the cow down until Bud could get out of the way.

With the head rope removed, I loosened the slack in my rope. The cow just laid there. Bud walked over and kicked the cow on the rump, and the cow promptly got up and she was on the fight. She tried to take Bud, but Sally quickly moved her horse in between Bud and the cow.

With Sally's big horse between Bud and the cow, the cow decided to leave Bud alone. I think the kick Sally placed on the cow's nose helped change the cow's intentions.

"Thank you, daughter," Bud said, as he walked past Sally and patted her on the knee.

"Daughter! That's what she was to Bud," I thought. "That's why she can do anything she wants to on this place!" I made up my mind to question her about this.

"It's almost lunch time," Bud said to the guests. "We'd better head back before the cook gets mad. This has been a successful branding, nobody got hurt, and we branded fifty-two calves, and doctored one cow. Sally roped seventeen calves and this young man roped thirty-five. The guests didn't rope any!"

Bud's last comment brought a laugh from the tourists. "But you'll have a chance to get even. I figure we've still got fifty or sixty calves to brand in the next couple of days."

The ride back to the ranch was uneventful. I did manage to

get close to Sally and say to her, "I didn't know you were Bud's daughter. I guess that's why you've got the run of the ranch an' can do anything you want."

"I can't do anything I want," she corrected me, "only what needs to be done."

"You appear to know what needs to be done. You're quite a hand." My compliment was meant to get me in her good graces, but it was a true comment. She was a good hand and that only comes from a lifetime of doing what she was doing, especially at our young ages.

"Thank you," was her only comment.

After lunch, which I was raised up calling dinner, Bud came up to me.

"Get your personal horse caught up," he said.

Before he finished I jumped to the conclusion that he was going to throw me off the place because I showed an interest in his daughter and he didn't like it.

"The horseshoer is coming and your horse needs shoeing," he said, as my mind was racing in other directions.

Relieved, I could only say, "Yes sir!"

I went to catch Roman. He was at the far end of the pasture and as I led him to the corral, I could hear the loose shoe. Sally and Sassy followed a short distance behind Roman. I thought Sally might need a trimming, but I didn't think she'd need shoes. Her hooves were dark and appeared to be in good shape. I decided I'd let the horseshoer make that decision.

The horseshoer arrived and promptly set up his anvil and equipment.

"Is this the horse I'm supposed to start on?"

"I guess so," I said.

The other wranglers were starting to catch Bud's horses that needed resetting.

"I've never shod this horse," said the shoer. "What's he like?"

"He'll stand pretty good," I said. I started to say that I've shod him in the past, but quickly shut up.

The shoer was picking up Roman's feet and inspecting them. He was saying, "Whoever shod this horse in the past sure didn't know what he was doing!"

I was glad I kept my mouth shut!

The horseshoer went right to work on Roman, pulling the old shoes, trimming the feet, selecting a shoe, shaping it and nailing it on. I was amazed at how fast he was, he was done in about an hour. It would have taken me half a day at least to get all four shoes on.

When he got done, I asked him about Sally. He looked at the burro's feet. "She doesn't really need anything done," he said.

I took Roman and Sally back to the pasture and turned them loose. I was content that I would be able to continue my trip with my animal's feet in good shape. When I returned to the horseshoer, Bud and his daughter had brought a thermos of cold lemonade and some cups down. Sally, the daughter, had even brought a cup for me.

Enlightened by Sally's obvious concern for me, my spirits were elevated.

Bud came over to me. "Our guests were quite impressed by your roping this morning. Would you and Sally like to give a clinic on roping for them this afternoon?"

"I don't know about a clinic," I said.

"It doesn't have to be that formal," said Bud. "We'll call it a clinic, but you just have to give them a few tips and let them practice. We've already set up a couple of dummies and got some extra lariat ropes up by the swimming pool."

"I guess we could do that," I said. The idea of Sally and me doing something together made the idea more appealing.

I went to my saddle, got my own lariat rope, and followed Bud and Sally up to the swimming pool.

The individuals wanting to rope were gathered around a table with a pitcher of lemonade on it.

"I suppose it would be good to start at the beginnin'," I said, as I handed out the ropes. "We'll start by buildin' a loop. The mistake most folks made this morning is that they made their loop to small. You need to make your loop at least big enough to catch what you're tryin' to catch, but not so big that the critter will run right through it, before you can jerk up your slack."

I demonstrated the proper size loop.

"Next," I said, "you need to move your hand back down the rope a good foot or so away from the honda. Doin' this will help keep your loop open."

"What's a honda?"

"That's this knot at the end of the rope," said Sally, holding the honda up to demonstrate. "The honda is what makes your loop when you put the end of the rope through it."

I could tell Sally was going to be a big help as I looked over our students. For the first time I noticed that the students were mostly ten- or twelve-year-old kids. The older kids and parents were hanging back, not participating, but listening and watching. I wondered if I was going too fast for them.

"Next," I continued, "you need to twirl the rope around your head like this." I demonstrated and each one of the kids attempted it.

One youngster ended up with his rope around himself. "I roped me!" he exclaimed.

Sally went over to help the youngster out of his rope.

"My dad roped himself this morning," said the youngster.

"Yes," said Sally. "You're already just as good as your dad. When we get done, you'll be better than he is."

Sally seemed to have a knack for saying just the right thing at just the right time.

"When you twirl that rope around your head, you need to have a flexible wrist and your fingers need to flex with the rope. You need to hold that rope like a finely tuned musical instrument, rather than a grip like you were holding a baseball bat," I said.

"Then, when you throw it, throw it just like you were throwing a baseball, right at the target. Throw the whole thing, so your loop will open up an' you can catch what you're throwin' at.

"Then, if you catch what you're throwin' at, jerk your slack, like this." I was demonstrating the actions as I talked. "If you catch what you're throwin' at, take your dallies an' you got your critter caught."

I simulated dallying up on an imaginary saddle horn in front of me.

I walked over to the dummy I was throwing at, took the rope off and continued. "If you miss your target, you coil your rope like this, making sure you twist the rope as you bring it in. These are hard twist ropes and you need to twist them like this so they will lay right on your saddle and in your hand when you're using them. Now, you kids practice."

I stepped out of the way, and Sally moved back so the kids had plenty of room to throw their ropes.

"You kids make sure you only rope the dummy," said Sally. "Don't be roping each other. Those ropes hurt when they hit you."

"But my sister's a dummy," said one of the boys.

"That's okay," said Sally. "Just don't be roping her."

I helped myself to some lemonade and stood back to watch my students practice. I didn't know how good my instructions were and from the predicament some of my students were in, my instructions weren't very good. Sally was right in there helping the kids untangle themselves and coiling their ropes. She had her hands full.

I put my lemonade down and went to help her. I saw a grateful look on her face as I approached and I heard her telling one of the youngsters, "It's okay, it takes a lot of practice to learn how to rope. Just keep trying!"

I helped untangle some of the kids and offered up encouragement just like I had heard Sally do. In fact, I said the same things.

Some of the youngsters were having small degrees of success at throwing the rope and a few would have caught the dummy if it would have had horns. One youngster did catch the dummy and was elated.

"Bet you can't do it again," came the comment from a discouraged kid.

"Just keep practicing," I said. "You'll get better."

I tried to be as encouraging as Sally and just as patient, but she was better at this than I was and I was getting tired and losing my patience. I found myself wishing the kids would get tired.

Finally the kids started to get tired and it wasn't long before we didn't have a class of kids any more.

"Any of you adults want to learn?" I was hoping they would

say no. Nobody volunteered and I was relieved. I got my rope and started to go to the barn to put it on my saddle and Sally followed.

"You were wonderful," she said.

"I don't know about that," I answered. "Those kids about wore me out. You were the one that showed the kids patience and each one of them got your personal attention. No, you were fantastic!"

I put my rope on my saddle and wanting to change the topic, I asked her, "What's the plan for tonight?"

"Nothing after supper. We can't keep these guests busy all the time; they need some time to relax."

I was relieved that there wasn't going to be another square dance. Going to bed early was beginning to look very inviting.

"What about tomorrow?"

"Tomorrow we've got to gather another pasture, and brand those calves the next day. Then our branding will be over for this year."

"Then the day after that, I'll leave," I blurted out. I didn't really mean to say it, but it was in my plans. I really wasn't used to catering to the dudes, and the social pressures were getting to me.

Wishing I hadn't said what I had, I hurriedly tried to change the subject. "How come you brand so late in the season?"

"That's so most of our guests get a chance to get involved in the branding. They generally only spend a week at a time here. Consequently, we try to schedule our brandings throughout the whole summer so almost everyone will have the opportunity to participate. Do you really have to leave? I think my dad wants you to stay on for another week or so."

Sally looked a little disappointed that I was leaving. I was feeling a little regret also. I didn't ask her if she wanted me to stay.

"I've got it in my mind to be home in time for school and school starts pretty soon. I've got some things to do before school starts."

"Dad says if you stayed, he could take a day, load up your stuff and your animals in the two-ton truck and take you home. He says it's only about a hundred miles or so. You could help us out here and still get home in time for school."

"I'll have to talk to your dad," I said.

"Okay," said Sally. "After supper would be a good time. See you then."

Sally left and I pondered my situation. I wasn't all that much against staying, in fact I thought I could enjoy Sally's company longer. Being late for school wouldn't bother me, but I might have a good talking to from my dad. But my trip had become an objective.

After supper, Bud looked me up.

"Sally told me you wanted to talk to me."

"Yes sir," I said. "After we brand what calves are left to brand, I'll pull out the next morning."

"Sally told me your plans and I had hoped you would stay an extra week or so."

"Yes sir," I said again. I was becoming very formal, probably because I didn't want to leave. "Sally also told me that you'd haul me and my animals home if I did stay. And I do appreciate that. But if I was to go home in a truck, it would look like to me anyways, and everyone else, that I had failed. I need to ride home just as I had originally intended and planned."

"I know how you feel and I understand," said Bud. "You do what you think you have to do."

We shook hands. "You know," he said, "you remind me a lot of myself when I was younger. Oh, by the way, I talked to your dad last night. He said that your mother's worried sick, she hasn't heard anything from you all summer."

"How did you talk to my dad?"

"By telephone, of course," said Bud, smiling.

Telephone! I'd been away from civilization for so long I'd forgotten all about the telephone. I felt guilty that I hadn't called my folks when I was in town at the rodeo, but getting hurt a little and then getting my animals stolen had kept me pretty busy.

I asked, "How did you know where to call?"

"Apparently, your old boss called your folks when you left that job. He gave your dad the name of the sheriff in that town, and your dad called the sheriff. Then, when you met up with my brother Fred, the forest ranger, he called the sheriff then he called me a couple of days before you showed up. We were actually expecting you when you got here. Your folks had a pretty good idea of where you were most of the time.

"When you got here, seeing as you didn't try to make contact with your folks, I called them just to let them know you were all right. I told your dad my plan about using you here for a few days, then bringing you home, and he said that you made your own decisions, whatever you wanted was all right with him. But you had to be home before Labor Day because school starts the day after Labor Day."

I thought I was doing all right and it was a surprise to me that I was being watched and tracked, at least over the phone. Oh well, I was still on my own. And I still had time to make it home in time for school.

"When's Labor Day?"

"You have ten days," answered Bud. "I could use you here for that, and then take you home."

"No," I said. "I need to stick to my original plan. If I go the way I've got planned, it will be about a hundred miles to get home."

"I can draw you a map and show you some shortcuts," said Bud. "It will shorten up your trip by about twenty or twenty-five miles."

"I'd sure appreciate that," I said. "That would save two or three days."

I was up early the next morning, but couldn't help gather the horses. They hadn't kept in a jingle horse for me. I was content to drink my coffee and watch Sally and the other hands bring in the horses.

We gathered cattle that day, and it was a tough day. The cattle were in a big pasture and it was rough country. We didn't stop for dinner, that is, lunch. The cook had made everyone a sandwich or two and we ate on the go. It was well past three o'clock when we turned the cattle into the pasture we'd turned the cattle into two days before.

We rode back to the ranch, tired dudes on tired horses. Even the hired help was a little tired. I know I was. That had been a tough pasture to gather. After supper, the only people that weren't tired were those that had opted to go fishing. Everyone else hit the sack early.

As I lay in my bedroll that night, I was thinking. "One more day, and the day after I would leave." I did have some regret and remorse about leaving, particularly leaving Sally. I wondered how I would react when I left and I wondered how she would react. I had a hard time getting to sleep and when I did, I spent a somewhat restless night and didn't sleep well.

The next day, it was apparent that all the guests were a little tired from the day before. I was a little tired, not having slept well. Some of the guests opted to not join the gather; they would ride out in the pickup with the cook when he brought out lunch. This was a little different than the procedure from a couple of days before, and as we rode out to start, I asked Bud about it.

"Yes, we did change our plans a little. I noticed that most of our guests were pretty tired yesterday, so I decided to make things easier on them. We always have to remember that these guests are what allows us to stay in the cattle business! Are you still planning on leaving tomorrow?"

"Yes," I said, "that's my plan."

"I'll bring you down some groceries tonight after supper. There's no sense in you leaving until after breakfast. You've gotten to know some of these people and they'll certainly want to say their goodbyes."

We got to the pasture where we had left the cattle the day before and started to gather the cattle. I was already familiar with this pasture, having helped gather it before and it was fairly simple to drive the cattle to the corral.

A fire had been built, the irons were getting hot and we were just about ready to get started.

Once again, I was selected to rope. None of the guests wanted to rope so Bud took a turn. I was amazed at how well he roped, in fact I was amazed at how well this whole family did everything.

I roped my first calf, but only had one hind foot.

"Both hind feet," said Bud, grinning, as I dragged the calf to the fire.

"I need a couple of loops to warm up," I said, trying to make an excuse for my lack of expertise. A feeble excuse, but it was the best I could come up with.

That was the same thing Sally had said when I'd dragged a

calf in by a hind foot a couple of days before. I thought I knew where she'd got it from.

The branding went well that morning and after Bud had roped ten or twelve calves, he gave his rope to one of the guests to let him try. The guest didn't have much success, and soon handed the rope back to Bud.

Bud then told Patrick to come out and rope a few. Patrick said he would, but only until Sally showed up. I was surprised at how good Patrick was. Everyone in this outfit, at least the hired help, was a good hand. I began to wonder if I was good enough to fit in with them. I hadn't seen Bud miss a loop, so far Patrick hadn't missed a loop, and I didn't remember Sally missing a loop a few days before. I'd missed some loops, and although I wasn't embarrassed, I thought every one of the hands on this place, including Sally, was a better hand than I was. It looked like to me that every hand on the place could do anything that needed to be done, without being told and without an argument. That, to me, was a sign of a well-managed, well-run outfit.

I thought to myself, "I'll certainly have to get a lot better if I'm going to associate with these people in the future!"

Presently, Sally showed up, and Patrick willingly gave up his roping position in favor of her. I volunteered to give her my position, but Patrick insisted he give up his spot, saying, "You might need some more practice."

I continued to rope and watch Sally at the same time. Finally, she missed a loop. I noticed the disgusted look on her face as she built another loop, but I didn't hear any vocalization of her disgust. I did notice a big grin on Bud's face as he witnessed her miss. I saw the same big smile on Patrick's face. I wondered what was happening.

I caught another calf and dragged him to the fire. "I noticed your amusement when Sally missed a calf," I said.

"Yes," said Bud. "She'll miss one every now and then, and that's good for her."

"Yep," said Patrick, "she's good, but we don't want her thinking she's better than she is."

"Well, she looks pretty good to me," I said.

"Yes," said Bud, laughing at the thinly disguised double meaning. Patrick was also laughing.

I thought to myself, "Was our friendship becoming something more and was it becoming that obvious?"

I didn't know. I certainly hadn't intended anything to develop, but did realize that I was getting a little warm. Then I realized that I was blushing. I hoped no one would notice, after all I did have a pretty deep suntan.

Before long Bud called a break in the branding. "Time to eat," he said. "The cows can set until after we eat."

I didn't realize it until Bud had mentioned it, but I was a little hungry and quite thirsty.

The cook had showed up with hot fried chicken and plenty of cold lemonade.

"This place certainly knows how to take care of people," I thought, as I sat down next to the corral. I leaned up against a corral post and started to eat when Sally joined me.

"You're a real good roper," I said. "I think you've only missed one loop in two days of roping."

"I shouldn't have missed that one," she said. "I just couldn't get my slack fast enough. You men," she continued, "why do you insist on eating in the worst areas? Come over here, get out of the dust."

The cattle were moving in the corral and the dust they were stirring up was drifting right over to where I was sitting.

She moved to a place out of the dust and I obediently followed, painfully aware that everyone was watching. Strangely, I felt much like a little lost puppy dog must have felt when he finally got home.

Lunch being done, it was time to get back to branding.

"Cookie," said Bud, "you want to rope some before you go back? There's only eight or ten left and there's no rush to get back."

"I guess I could," said the cook, "if you don't mind cold cuts for supper."

"Holy cow," I thought, "everyone on this outfit is a cowboy, including the girl and the cook."

"Better rope," said Bud. "Some of those calves have been thrown at and missed—they might be a little wild."

I was sure Bud's comment was a reference to my roping, but I saw Sally start to blush and wasn't sure if his comment was a dig at her, me, or both of us.

"Use my horse," continued Bud. "We can shorten the stirrups, but don't you forget to put them back where they belong! Last time we did this, I had to get off halfway home and adjust my stirrups. I almost got saddle sore!"

"Yea boss," said the cook, as he took off his apron.

I volunteered to sit out, content to watch Sally rope. I did take on the loud-mouthed teenager's job of holding down the front end of the calves while they were branded, vaccinated, earmarked, and castrated. I didn't have near the problem he had, but I'd done this before.

I was surprised at how well the cook roped. It was evident he'd done this before and more than once. He did bring in one calf he'd caught by one hind leg, and I was going to harass him some, but didn't get the chance. Before I could say anything, Bud and Sally both said, "Two hind legs!" They were both grinning as they said it.

"You complain about my ropin' an' I'll give you somethin' to really complain about at supper," replied the cook.

"If we're having cold cuts, I'm ready to start complaining now," said Bud.

"Me too," said Patrick.

"Ah, shut up," replied the cook. "We ain't having cold cuts an' I got some more calves to rope before we're done. You just do your work there on the ground an' I'll finish doing your horseback work!"

"Don't make the cook mad," hollered one of the dudes, "We still gotta eat tonight!"

The good-natured kidding and ribbing that seemed to be going on all the time made this a nice place to be. I started to regret a little more the fact that I was leaving tomorrow.

It wasn't long before we were done. The cook had loaded up his supplies and departed. The ride back to the ranch was slow and peaceful. We were riding along in groups of twos and threes just taking our time. I was riding at the rear of the group, watching how some of the dudes sat on their horses and wondering how they would act when they left, after a week of horseback riding on a dude ranch. I wondered if they would still try to imitate the walk of Bud and Patrick. The cook even had the same walk—he'd been horseback quite a bit in his life.

I hadn't noticed, but Sally had been slowing her horse down a little, visiting with the guests as they rode past her. Next thing I knew, she was riding right next to me.

"What are you doing riding back here all by yourself?"

"Just thinking," I replied.

"About what?"

"Well," I said, "I'm leavin' in the mornin'. I've got to get packed up an' get an early start. Its goin' to be a little difficult to leave tomorrow, I've had more fun here than I've had all summer."

"I'm glad to hear that! What are your plans for next summer?"

I was thinking, "This girl could sure ask a lot of questions," as I answered her. "I really don't have any plans made. I need to get through school before I start making any definite plans."

"Are you a good student?"

"Not really," I said. "My grades are passing but not outstanding. I have to keep them up to stay on the rodeo team, and for me that's a lot of work."

"So your grades are good because of the rodeo team?"

"Just passable, I suppose."

"What rodeo events do you compete in?"

More questions. I had to figure out how to ask some of my own questions.

"I ride the three rough stock events and do some team ropin' when I can get a partner an' some practice. What are your plans?"

"I plan on going to college."

I asked, "Where?"

"I don't know yet. I hope to get a scholarship. I have to graduate from high school first."

"Are your grades that good?" I was beginning to think I was out of my league.

"For the most part," she replied. "I do have some problems in math."

I couldn't think of anything else to say, so I just rode along, quiet.

Presently, Sally said, "You could get a job next summer

working for my dad. He says you're a good hand, and you know livestock."

"I ain't too good around people," I said.

"Oh, that's no big thing. Misses Abercrombie says she likes you just the way you are, a little rough around the edges."

"You mean lacking in the social graces, I suppose."

"Call it whatever you want," she said, "but the guests have all taken a liking to you. It wouldn't be hard for you to fit in."

"But I don't even know how to square dance," I said, remembering how confused I got at the dance a couple of nights ago.

"I could teach you, if you wanted to learn."

Sally seemed more than anxious to teach me, this was her second offer.

"Do you always have as much fun around here as you appear to?"

"Generally, yes. Dad is pretty easy going until it's time to sell the calves and make the bank payment. But he says it's been getting easier every year."

We were reaching the ranch and had rode on without saying much more.

When we got to the ranch, Sally unsaddled her horse and headed for the lodge. Before she left, she said, "You think about next summer!"

I helped the dudes off and helped unsaddle the horses. I'd learned some of the horses' names and could put their saddles away in the proper places. Those horses I didn't know, Patrick was kind enough to tell me their names. When we got done, I unsaddled Drygulch and turned him loose.

"You're a good horse," I said, as I patted him on the rump and walked away. "You might be worth comin' back for next summer."

Patrick heard me. "You figuring on coming to work next

summer? Bud told me he was going to offer you a job for next year. Would you be coming back for Drygulch or Sally?"

He laughed and I became embarrassed.

"I don't know," I said. I was kind of stammering and stuttering at the frankness of Patrick. "I'd better go get cleaned up for supper."

I was kind of uncomfortable. Things were happening fast and I wasn't sure what was happening.

In the shower, I decided, as fast as things were happening, it might be best to leave the next morning. At least, out on the trail, I could sort things out and figure out how I fit in this mess.

I got dressed in the cleanest clothes I had, although they were wrinkled, and started toward the lodge. Sally met me halfway with a sack in her hand.

"Dad is giving you these."

She handed me the sack. Inside was a new pair of pants and a new shirt. They were both the right size.

"How'd he know the size?"

"You've got it printed on the tab of your pants," said Sally. "He just guessed at the shirt. He thought you might want to look good at your last supper ... that is, your last night."

The religious reference was obvious and I had to laugh.

"I'll go back an' change," I said.

"I'll go with you," she said.

"No," I said, becoming embarrassed at the thought of Sally watching me change clothes. "You go to the lodge, I'll meet you there."

"I'll go as far as the bunkhouse," she said. "I'll wait outside while you change." She was aware of my embarrassment and was chuckling to herself.

Feeling safe, I consented.

Supper was roast beef, ranch-raised I was told. It was a lot better than the cold cuts the cook had promised earlier in the day.

After supper, Sally suggested I walk around and tell everyone goodbye.

"Is that necessary?"

"Yes it is," replied Sally. "It will help improve your social graces."

She took my hand and began to lead me around to the guests so I could talk to everyone. I was embarrassed, and I thought of a lamb being led to slaughter. "Maybe," I thought, "her comment about your last supper isn't too far off!"

I made my goodbyes as brief as possible. I was surprised at how many people told me they'd be up to see me off. Even Misses Abercrombie, who I had started to like a little, said she'd be down to see me leave.

Still holding my hand, Sally led me around to each guest and then to her dad.

"I can see you're determined to leave," he said.

"Yes sir," I answered.

"Sally told me she offered you a job next summer."

"Yes sir," I answered again.

"Are you going to take it?"

"I don't know. A lot can happen between now and then. While I'm thinkin' of it, I do want to thank you for the clothes. They fit perfect."

"Yes, I knew they would. You think about this job we're offering you. I'll need to know by the middle of March, we have a lot of job applicants for our summer positions. Most of them aren't qualified, but you are. You could be a big help to us and we might even have a couple of colts you could start. I know Sally wants you to come back."

He smiled as he made the last comment and Sally started to blush. I was starting to blush, too, at least I felt like it. It was apparent he was enjoying this.

"Here," he said, handing me an envelope. "This is your pay for giving us a hand and helping out."

"But this shirt an' pants is plenty," I protested. "I didn't do all that much anyways."

"Take it," said Bud. "It's worth it to me. You gave these dudes, er … guests plenty to talk about the last few days."

I took the envelope and put it in my pocket without opening it up and counting it. It occurred to me that I'd put other money in my pocket as I jammed the envelope in the pocket, and didn't even know how much money I had.

"Here's a map of the easiest way for you to get home. I've marked an "X" at where you should camp each day. There's good water at all those camps. The third day out you'll come onto the Peterson Ranch. I talked to them and you can cross their property without any trouble. They're good people.

"A day after that, you'll be on Forest Service property. Two, maybe two-and-a-half days later, you'll come into Peaceful Valley."

"Peaceful Valley! I know that country! That's home," I interrupted.

"Yes, I know. You should know that you'll only have about three-quarters of a day's ride until you're home. When you get home, tell your dad I said hello."

"You *know* my dad?"

"Yes," answered Bud, "I met him at a cow sale some years ago and I bought some of his yearlings for replacement heifers."

"I didn't see any cattle with our brand on 'em when we branded," I said.

"The cattle we got from you were all early calvers. We branded their calves last spring. You'll probably see some of them before you leave our property.

"The cook has some stuff for you in the kitchen. Make sure you pick it up before you leave. Also, there's a half a sack of grain down at the barn. Take it for your horse and burros, it should be enough to get them home."

I was flabbergasted. All I could say was, "Thank you!"

Sally still had my hand. "I'll take you to the kitchen," she said.

The cook had two grocery sacks sitting on the counter.

"Take that stuff an' get out of my kitchen," he said. I think he was trying real hard to be gruff.

I picked up a sack. It was heavy and I knew it was canned goods.

"I'll take this one," said Sally.

"I can get it," I said.

"I'll get it," said Sally, and picked it up.

"I hope its lighter than this one," I said.

"It is," she said.

We carried the sacks to the bunkhouse. Sally came right in like she owned the place, at least like her dad did, and he did, and set the sack on the bunk.

I set my bag down and started to unload the sack.

"What are you doing?"

"I've got to get this stuff in the panniers as even as I can, so I'm ready to go in the morning," I said.

"I'll help you," she said, and promptly started unloading the sack she brought down.

I got the panniers, unloaded them and started to repack them, trying to get the weight as even as possible in each pannier. When I was satisfied, I told Sally, "That's it. All I have to do

121

is saddle up, load the panniers on Sally, the other Sally that is, an' I'm ready to go."

"Then walk with me," she said.

She took my hand and led me out the door. It was starting to get dark and I thought she wanted me to escort her to her quarters. I thought this was nice, I was lacking in my social skills and she was giving me the opportunity to be a gentleman and improve my skills. I was surprised when we headed toward the barn rather than the lodge and she still had a hold of my hand.

It was dark in the barn, and if Sally wasn't still holding my hand, I'm sure I would have run away.

"I really don't want you to go," she said.

"I really need to …" I started to say. She silenced me by putting a finger to my lips.

"I know you're too bashful to say or do anything with other people around, so I'm going to kiss you goodbye right here and get a promise from you that at least you'll write every now and then."

She put both her arms around my neck and placed her lips on mine. I backed up wondering if I should try to escape, and she soon had me pinned against the wall. Instinctively, I put my arms around her and felt her moist mouth on mine. I wondered what I should do. I didn't know what to do, so I didn't do anything. I just stood there and endured.

I wondered how long I was going to have to endure what I was going through. This wasn't at all like what I had seen in the movies.

Presently, Sally released her grip on me and backed off. I was free and wanted to run away and wipe the slobber off my mouth. I didn't do either one—I just stood there, quivering a little. I didn't think I *could* run—I felt a little weak in the knees.

"You haven't kissed many girls, have you?"

"Well, ah … no, I ah …"

"I didn't think so," she said. "That's something we can work on next summer. Make sure you write me. Here's my address."

She handed me a folded piece of paper, and started to leave.

"I should at least walk you up to the lodge," I said.

"I know the way better than you," she said. And she left.

I had the feeling that she was sorely disappointed as I watched her walk in the darkness to the lodge.

My knees returned to normal and I went to the bunkhouse.

I felt strange—I had kissed a girl, for the first time! On second thought, I concluded I hadn't kissed a girl, I had been kissed by a girl. Sally had been in control of the situation from the start.

On the Trail Again

The next morning, I was up early. I grabbed a handful of grain and a halter and went out to catch Roman. I hadn't been giving Roman or Sally any grain the last couple of days, our routine had been changed to some degree and they weren't coming in for grain.

The wranglers hadn't brought the horses in yet, it was still pretty early.

I led Roman to the barn and Sally and Sassy followed. I saddled Roman and Sally and was about ready to take Sally to the bunkhouse and get her packed when Bud showed up.

"Better go to the kitchen and get some breakfast," he said. "At least the coffee's ready."

"I can do that," I said. A cup of coffee before I left did sound appealing.

I was surprised to find Sally in the kitchen with the cook.

"I thought you'd be out gathering horses this morning," I said.

"No," she said, as she poured me a cup of coffee. "I do have some other things to do."

As I sipped my coffee, I watched her. There was something different about her today, but I couldn't put my finger on it. I was really hoping she wouldn't say anything about last night, I was already feeling selfconscious.

A dress! She was wearing a dress. That's what was different. I hadn't seen her in a dress before and she did look nice. It never did occur to me that girls had legs, I hadn't really paid any attention.

I finished my coffee and started toward the bunkhouse to pack Sally.

"Swing by here when you leave, so everyone can say goodbye," said Bud.

"Yes sir."

I got Sally packed, looked around the bunkhouse one more time to make sure I hadn't left anything, then tied Sassy to Sally. I got on Roman, gathered up Sally's lead rope and started out. I made a swing by the lodge and was surprised to see Bud, Sally, and most of the guests on the porch. Some of them had their cameras and were taking my picture. I was painfully aware of how much my outfit resembled some gypsy outfit and anxious to get out of the limelight. I didn't really like being the center of attention.

I stopped in front of the lodge. "It's been nice meetin' you folks," I said. "You all take care an' we'll see you again sometime."

I waved a goodbye amidst their goodbyes and wishes of "Good luck!"

Sally, the burro, had her nose to the ground looking for something to eat. I jerked her head up, said, "Sally, you ol' hussy, let's go!"

This brought a laugh from the group, and I started out. I rode about a hundred yards, turned to wave one more time and noticed Bud holding Sally around the shoulder. Sally appeared to have her head buried in Bud's chest. Was she crying? I couldn't tell at this distance.

I didn't know. I didn't have time for such childish stuff. I rode on, and after another hundred yards, looked around again. The crowd had pretty much left and Bud was taking Sally into the lodge, his arm still around her shoulder and, as near as I could tell, her head still buried in his chest.

I rode on, wondering if I should turn around and go back to see what was wrong. But I kept going. I wasn't sure, but I suspected that I had something to do with whatever was happening. I dismissed any thoughts that I might have such a profound effect on Sally. And why was Sally wearing a dress? Was it because of me? I hadn't even said anything about how nice she looked. Social graces! I certainly needed more work in that area!

I rode on, feeling a little more forlorn with each step Roman took. I hadn't really felt this way before and didn't know how to act. I took out the map Bud had drawn for me and started to study it, trying to get my mind off leaving the outfit and Sally.

It didn't do much good, and my feelings were betraying me. Maybe I wasn't as grown up as I thought I was.

"Come on, Sally," I said, as I jerked her head up again. But when I looked at her, I didn't see the donkey, I saw a pretty girl, about my age, with long blonde hair fixed in a ponytail, with blue eyes shining, looking back at me, smiling.

"I think we're goin' to have to change you're name," I told her. "It just doesn't seem quite respectable to call you her name."

I spent time trying to think of a new name for my burro, but my thoughts kept wandering back to Sally. I knew I wasn't making good time and decided I'd have to put the situation behind me and start paying attention to what I was doing.

"Matilda! That's your new name Sally! You better get used to it," I told her.

The day passed slowly. I had more thinking to do, but was distracted by thoughts of Sally. Actually, I *was* thinking about Sally, I couldn't get her out of my mind.

I made camp that night, careful to give Roman and Matilda an extra feed of grain. I wanted them to be close to camp the next morning. Our routine had changed some and I wanted to resume our original procedures.

Supper was the same that night and I wondered if Cookie's good cooking hadn't spoiled me.

I was up early the next morning and on the move. I was feeling somewhat better, but still thinking about Sally—quite a bit about her to be honest.

"Whoever said, 'Parting is such sweet sorrow,' didn't know what he was talking about," I told Matilda as we traveled.

I did see some cattle that had my dad's brand as I passed by. They all had big calves by their sides, and I noticed a slick calf or two. The slicks were earmarked, but not branded.

"They wouldn't have got past Sally an' me if we'd have been at their brandin'," I told Roman.

I noticed I was including Sally in a lot of my comments as I talked to my horse and burros. I had assumed we were a team, even though we were separated. I thought it might be a lot of fun to help Bud gather all his cattle later that fall, especially with Sally to help.

A couple of day's more riding and I left Bud's property and entered the Peterson ranch.

The second day on their ranch I met some of the Peterson hands and Mister Peterson. I declined an invitation to spend the night at their ranch, preferring to stick as close as I could to the map Bud had drawn for me. And, I thought if I got involved in helping the Peterson's, I might lose another day. Bud was right, the Peterson's were good people.

A couple of days in the forest and I entered Peaceful Valley. My trip was almost over. I knew that I was about to enter the world I had left earlier in the summer. I entered our ranch, and saw some of our cattle. They looked good, they had done all right without my help all summer. I rode past some of our hay fields and noticed that the hay was about ready to cut.

I rode to the barn to unsaddle Roman and Matilda. I met my dad in the barn. He was changing the oil in the tractor, getting ready to cut the third crop of hay.

"You made it," he said, sticking out his hand to shake. I hadn't been greeted with a handshake by my dad before. I shook his hand and felt strangely equal.

"I understand you've picked up some livestock," he said. "Let's see what you've got."

We walked outside so Dad could look at my horse and burros. The pack on Matilda had shifted a little and I was a little embarrassed as Dad surveyed the situation.

"Looks like a pretty fair horse, although he's a little on the small side."

"He's good enough for me," I said. "I used him all summer before I traded for him."

I started to unpack Matilda before Dad could say anything about my unbalanced load. I still thought my outfit resembled a wandering gypsy, and was slightly embarrassed.

"What's the story on the burros?" Dad was casting a stockman's practiced eye at Matilda and Sassy.

"Part of the trade," I said. "I needed something to pack my bedroll an' supplies on. The colt came along after we started.

She did all right, although I may have overloaded a time or two. That was the best I could do."

I knew Dad was figuring out the value of Matilda in his head but he didn't say anything other than, "Just a couple of burros."

I thought he thought they weren't worth much.

"What you going to do with them?"

"Now that I'm home, I don't know. I haven't given it any thought." I'll have to admit I had become attached to them during our travels.

"Turn them loose in the horse pasture," said Dad. "Your mother is up at the house fixing supper along with your brothers and sister. Your mother will be glad to see you, she's been worried sick about you since you left your job."

I had one younger sister and four younger brothers. I thought it a little strange that I hadn't given them a thought all summer. While I knew they were my brothers and sister, it was almost like I had completely forgot them. I hadn't even told Sally about them.

I finished unpacking Matilda and turned her, Sassy and Roman into the horse pasture. I got my bedroll and started toward the house. My mother met me on the porch.

"Don't be coming in here with that bedroll," she said, "I'll bet it smells to high heaven!"

I dropped the bedroll and met Mom with a big hug. We went through the customary greetings and questions, although she was careful not to mention how worried she was while I had been gone.

"I have some leftover groceries an' supplies I have to bring up," I said. I was surrounded by my siblings, all volunteering to help, and they were asking questions about my trip as we carried my supplies to the house.

"Supper will be ready soon," said my mother. "You can tell us about your adventures at supper. You kids go get washed up. You, young man," she said pointing at me, "go get a shower!"

"But Mom, I had one a week ago!" I was kidding my mother, but she rarely found humor in my kidding.

"I'll bet it was longer than that! Go get in the shower, your clean clothes are in your room. I've even bought you some new school clothes."

I didn't think much of her buying me clothes. She always bought what she thought I should wear. I bought what I thought I would be comfortable in.

At supper, I related my adventures on the trail. My siblings were quite interested and Dad only showed a passing interest until I mentioned the part about the mountain lion.

"That lion was around here earlier this summer," he said. "He got one of our calves, but I couldn't get him. It's too bad that sheepherder didn't get him."

I told them about the jobs I had been offered and the rest of my adventures, but was careful not to mention Sally. When I got done, Dad asked, "What are your plans for next summer?"

"I'm thinkin' I'll probably go to work on that dude ranch," I said. "He's willin' to pay good money, there's a lot of ridin' an' he might even have a couple of colts for me to start." I was careful not to mention Sally, but she would be the main reason I'd go to work for Bud.

"By the way," said my mother, "this came for you the other day."

Mom got up and retrieved a letter from the mantle addressed to me. "It just got here day before yesterday."

I said, "Thank you," and put the letter in my pocket.

"Aren't you going to read it?" My little sister was curious and so was I. The envelope had the dude ranch's logo on it and the handwriting was obviously feminine.

"I'll get to it later," I said. I felt I was starting to blush a little and it was starting to get a little warm in the room.

"Are you sure Bud's daughter doesn't have anything to do with your decision?" Dad had a big smile on his face when he asked the question.

I had seen that amused look on Bud's face when he told me Sally had wanted me to come back next year. Was this a conspiracy?

"Bud told me that he knew you," I said, wanting to change the subject.

"I sold him some yearlings a few years ago, and I've talked to him on the phone a few times, quite a few times recently, in fact."

"I saw some cattle with our brand on them as I rode through his property," I said. "They looked pretty good and they all had calves at their side."

"He's a pretty shrewd businessman, and you can go to the bank on anything he says."

"What have you got planned the next couple of days?" I asked. I knew I was going to have to help out and I wanted to find out what I had to do tomorrow, so I could leave the table and read my letter. I knew who it was from.

"Now that you're here, we'll irrigate that far hay field, then start cutting hay, close to the house. We can get a lot of it down before school starts. What are your plans for the winter?"

"I guess I'll have to go to school. I think I need to improve my social skills and I want to learn how to square dance." I didn't say that I wanted to practice my kissing, but I needed to and didn't know just how to go about it.

Dad had a big smile on his face. "Then go to work for Bud in the spring?"

"I guess so," I said. I excused myself and went outside to read my letter.

The next morning, I found myself irrigating the far hay field. I was doing the same thing that I had been doing when I quit my former boss and started my trip! But it was okay. I had a letter from Sally in my pocket!